Hermann Sudermann, Elizabeth Lee, Lily Henkel

The Wish

A Novel

Hermann Sudermann, Elizabeth Lee, Lily Henkel

The Wish
A Novel

ISBN/EAN: 9783337349257

Printed in Europe, USA, Canada, Australia, Japan

Cover: Foto ©Andreas Hilbeck / pixelio.de

More available books at **www.hansebooks.com**

THE WISH

A NOVEL

BY

HERMANN SUDERMANN

TRANSLATED BY

LILY HENKEL

WITH A BIOGRAPHICAL INTRODUCTION BY

ELIZABETH LEE

NEW YORK

D. APPLETON AND COMPANY

1895

INTRODUCTION.

SINCE *the beginning of time men have been accustomed to regard the end of a century as a period of decadence. The waning nineteenth century is no more fortunate than its predecessors. We are continually being invited to speculate on the signs around us of decay in politics, in religion, in art, in the whole social fabric. It is not for us to inquire here concerning the truth or the ethics of that belief. But, as far as literature is concerned, it is very certain that the last years of the present century will be remembered for the extraordinary talent shown by a few young novelists and dramatists in most of the countries of Europe. In England, we can point to Mr. Rudyard Kipling and Mr. J. M. Barrie; in France, to M. Paul Margueritte and M. Marcel Prévost; in Belgium, to M. Maurice Maeterlinck;*

in Germany, to Gerhard Hauptmann, Ludwig Fulda, and Hermann Sudermann.

The events of Sudermann's life are few ; and he has the good sense to prefer to be known through his works rather than through the medium of the professional interviewer. The facts here set down, however, we owe to the courtesy of Sudermann himself, a circumstance that lends them an additional interest.

Hermann Sudermann was born September 30, 1857, at Matzicken, a poor village in Heydekrug, a district of East Prussia, situated on the Russian frontier. It is not unlikely that the following passage taken from one of his novels bears some resemblance to the place :—

" The estate that my father farmed was situated on a high hill close to the Prussian frontier ; an uncultivated, wild park sloping gently towards the open fields formed one side of the hill, while the other sank steeply down to a little river. On the farther side of the stream you could see a dirty little Polish frontier village.

" Standing at the edge of the precipice you looked down on the ruinous shingle roofs ; the smoke came up through the rifts in them. You looked right into the midst of the miserable life of the dirty streets where half-naked children wallowed in the filth, where the women squatted idly on the threshold, and where the men in torn smocks, with spade on shoulder, betook themselves to the alehouses.

" There was nothing attractive about the town, and the rabble of frontier Cossacks, who galloped here and there on their catlike, drowsy nags, did not increase the charm."

Sudermann began his education at the school of Elbing. But his parents were in poor circumstances, and at the age of fourteen he found it necessary to think about earning a living, and was apprenticed to a chemist. He continued his studies in his leisure time with such good results that he returned to school, this time at Tilsit. In 1875 he went to the university of Königsberg, and in 1877 to that of Berlin. His first intention was to become a teacher, and while still pursuing his studies undertook for a few months the duties of tutor in the house of the poet Hans Hopfen. But in 1881, after six years spent in studying history, philosophy, literature, and modern languages (Sudermann understands English perfectly), he turned to journalism, and edited *the* Deutsches Reichsblatt, *a political weekly.   He soon threw aside newspaper work for true literature, for what the Germans call* belletristik, *and he has become famous through his novels, short stories, and plays.   He is good-looking, with a dark melancholy face that lights up with a most remarkable and expressive smile when he speaks ; nothing could be more unaffected than his manner, nor more charming than his whole personality.   As yet there is no Sudermann Society for the discussion of the author's works, but in Berlin, where he has many admiring friends, Sudermann occasionally reads to them his productions while they are yet unpublished.   The little story called* Iolanthe's Hochzeit *was first heard in that way.*

Although Sudermann's work is in all its aspects essentially modern, indeed all the conditions and problems of modern life have the highest interest for him, he belongs to no class, ranges himself with neither realists nor idealists, and bows to the yoke of no literary fashion.   In common with all great artists, Sudermann paints his own age, but while portraying men and women as he knows them, in the nineteenth century, he gives them, at least in his novels and tales, the human nature that is the same through all time. He has lived in Berlin, and his dramas give us life in that city both among the proletariat and the rich middle class. He has lived in East Prussia, and there is laid the scene of his longer novels. He is familiar with other parts of Germany, with Italy, and with Paris, and everywhere he has used his gift of keen observation to good purpose. A certain melancholy, a feeling of the "inevitableness" of things, if we may be allowed the expression, runs through all his writings, and may perhaps be traced to the effect on his sensitive and high-strung nature of the East Prussian landscape, amid which he spent his boyhood. The meadow-flats and corn-lands, the meagre pine-woods, and dark, lonely pools of his native district, form the background of most of his tales. Numerous passages might be quoted which would serve to show the melancholy and loneliness of the landscape. As an example we may take :—

" Thick and heavy as if you could grasp them with your hands, the clouds spread over the flat land. Here and there the trunk of a willow stretched forth its rugged knots to the air, heavily laden with moisture. The tree was soaked with damp, and

glistened with the drops that had hung in rows on the bare boughs. The wheels sank deep into the boggy road that ran between withered reeds and sedge.

*　　*　　*　　*　　*

" The moon stood high in the heavens and shed her calm, bluish light far over the sleeping heath. The clumps of alders on the moor bore wreaths of light, and from the slender silvery trunks of the birches which bordered the broad straight road in endless rows, came a sparkle and brightness that made the road seem as if lost far below in the silvery distance.

" Silence all around. The birds had long ceased singing. A stillness of the late summer time, the complacent stillness of departing life lay over the broad plain. You scarcely heard the sound of a cricket in the ditches, or a field-mouse disturbed in its slumbers, gliding through the tall grass with its low chirping whistle."

Such pictures constantly meet us in the pages of Sudermann's books ; taken in connection with their setting, they are often of great force and beauty. Nothing, however, is obtruded ; there is no searching after a dramatic background, or undue word-

painting; everything is in keeping with and subordinate to the main interest of the tale.

With such surroundings, Sudermann cleverly assimilates his characters. They are mostly the victims of circumstances which they are more or less unable to overcome. In some cases the fault, as with Leo Sellenthin in Es war, *Sudermann's latest novel, lies in the weakness or sinfulness of the man; in others, in surroundings and events for which the man is not himself directly responsible. Sometimes the noble unselfish love and devotion of a woman make a happier state of things possible; Sudermann is a firm believer in the power and influence of good women in human life. His women are not so sharply outlined as Ibsen's, but he recognises in the sex, though much more vaguely, like possibilities. For example, Leonore in* Die Ehre *sees the folly and emptiness of fashionable life and has the courage to give her hand where she loves, to a man who, by her set, would be considered far beneath her. Magda, in* Heimat, *refuses to desert her child. And his young girls are even more charming, more natural than those of Ibsen. Eager-hearted Dina Dorf, with her desire for a larger life in the world; hard-*

working *Petra Stockman* with her delight in her work and her unflinching truth and honesty; *Bolette Wangel* with her desire for knowledge, "to know something about everything" are, as everybody knows, among *Ibsen's* most delightful creations. In Es War *Sudermann* gives us as perfect and natural a study of a young girl as we have met with in fiction or the drama for a very long while. *Hertha* cherishes a secret love for a man much older than herself but has reason to fear that his affections are set on a married woman, the wife of his best friend. To *Hertha's* innocent and unworldly mind this is a great puzzle; to her the sacredness of love between husband and wife seems a matter of course.

"*Certainly the beautiful woman was a thousand times lovelier than poor Hertha—and she was, moreover, much cleverer. . . . But could she—and therein lay the great puzzle, the invincible contradiction that knocked all suspicion on the head—could she as a married woman possibly be an object of love to a man other than her husband? Wives were loved by their husbands—that is why they are married—and by no one else in the world.*"

But Hertha determines to take such means as are within her power of discovering if such things are possible, if such things exist. She first consults her books—books, of course, suited to a young girl's library. She goes through her novels, but nothing in them points to the enormity. Then she turns to the classics, to Schiller!

" Amalie was a young girl—so was Luise—but then there was the queen of Spain! However, in that case it was clear as noonday how little poets deserved to be trusted, for that a man should fall in love with his stepmother could only take place in the world of imagination where genius, drawn away from the earth, intoxicated with inspiration, soars aloft. Not in vain had she, a year and a half before, written a school composition on ' Genius and Reality,' in which she had treated the question in a most exhaustive manner."

She next tries her friend Elly, a girl of her own age, but much more experienced in the ways of the world.

" ' Listen, dear, I want to ask you a very important question. You're in love, aren't you ? '

" ' Yes,' replied Elly.

"' *And you're sure the man's in love with you ?*'

"' *Why do you say* "*man*" *?*' *asked Elly.* ' *Curt is my ideal. A little time ago it was Bruno—and before that it was Alfred—but now it's Curt. Yet he's not a man.*'

"' *What is he, then ?*'

"' *He's a* young *man.*'

"' *Oh ! that's it, is it ? No, he's certainly not a man.* *And Hertha's eyes shone: she knew what a* ' *man*' *looked like.* ' *Well, darling,*' *she went on,* ' *do you think that a* "*man,*" *or a* young *man—it's all the same—could possibly love a married woman ?*'

"' *Of course—naturally he would,*' *replied Elly, with perfect calmness.*

" *Hertha smiled indulgently at such want of intelligence.*

"' *No, no, little one,*' *she said.* ' *I don't mean his own wife, but a woman who is the wife of another ?*'

"' *So do I,*' *replied Elly.*

"' *And that seems to you quite a matter of course ?*'

"' *My dear child, I didn't think you were so innocent,*' *said Elly ;* ' *everybody knows as much as that.   And formerly it was even worse.   A true knight always loved another man's wife: it was a great crime to love his own wife.   He would cut off his right hand for the stranger's sake, and would die for her, pressing her blue favour to his lips ; for you see at that time they always wore her blue favour. You'll find it in every history of literature.'*

" Hertha became very thoughtful.   'Ah! in those days!' she said, with the ghost of a smile; 'in those days men went to tournaments and stabbed each other in sport with their lances.'

"'And to-day,' whispered Elly, 'men shoot each other dead with pistols.'

" Hertha felt as if she had been stabbed to the heart, and the little pink and white daughter of Eve continued, 'I think it must be quite delightful when one is married to know that some one is hopelessly in love with you.   It's quite certain that most unhappy love affairs arise in that way.'

" The next day Hertha questioned her grandmother.

"' Grandmother, I'm grown up now, aren't I ?'

"' Yes—so, so,' answered the old lady.

"' And probably I shall soon be married ?'

"' You!' shouted her grandmother, in deadly

terror. Doubtless the wretched child had come to confide in her the addresses of some booby of a neighbour.

"'Yes,' continued Hertha, inarticulately and with great hesitation; 'with my big fortune I am not likely to be an old maid.'

"'Child!' exclaimed the old lady, 'of whom are you thinking?'

"Hertha blushed to her neck. 'I?' she stammered, trying to preserve an indifferent tone of voice, 'of nobody.'

"'Oh, then you were merely talking generally?'

"'Of course; I only meant generally.'

"'Well, and what do you want to know?'

"'I want to know—how it is with—you understand—with love when one——'

"'When one——'

"'Well, when one is married?'

"'Then you go on loving just as you did before,' replied her grandmother, lightly.

"'Yes, I know that. But suppose you love another man to whom you aren't married?'

"'Wha—t!' In her terror the old lady let her spectacles fall off her nose. 'What other?'

"*Hertha suddenly felt as if she must collapse. She had to summon all her courage and pull herself together in order to go on.*

"'*Can't it happen, grandmother dear, that some one to whom you're not married takes it into his head——*'

"'*My dear child,' replied the grandmother, 'never come to me with such foolish questions. You cannot understand such things. Now give me a kiss and get your knitting.'*"

So that plan did not answer. There was still one further possibility of discovery. Hertha had a school friend who had lately got married. She would ask her. So she began :—

"'*Wives love their husbands, that goes without saying. But do you think it possible that wives can be loved by other men ?*'

"'*How odd you are,' replied Meta. 'You can't prevent people loving.*'

"'*I know that. But a man, don't you see, who would——*'

"'*Well, that sort of thing does happen.*'

"'*What ! is some one in love with you ?*'

"*Meta blushed. 'I don't bother about it. It's*

2

quite enough that Hans loves me, and of course I should very politely forbid anything of the sort.'

   "' Then people do forbid such things ?'

   "' Certainly, if they're told of it.'

   "' What ! you might be told ?'

   "' Sometimes, if the man who is in love with you is very bold.'

   "' Good gracious,' said Hertha, shocked. 'If any-one behaved like that to me, I should box his ears.' But in great anxiety she continued, ' Do you think it likely that there are women who have a different opinion ? '

   "' Oh, yes !' said Meta.

   "' Who—in the end—return the bold man's love ?'

   "' Even so.'"

Then Meta repeats certain gossip that confirms Hertha's worst fears. The whole chapter should be read in order to appreciate rightly the charm and pathos and naturalness of the delightful piece of character drawing.

✓ Like Ibsen and Zola, Sudermann does not hesitate to set the truth before us even when it is terrible or brutal or revolting. But he differs from them in having a less gloomy outlook, in firmly believing that, at the

same time as human nature is coarse and brutal, stupid and violent, it is loving, capable of sacrifice and of deep feeling. He sees the strange not to say the inexplicable mixture of good and evil in all things human, and knows man to be neither all gold nor all alloy. This we take it is the true realism.

To make Sudermann's point of view clear to English readers there is perhaps no better nor more direct way than to give a brief account of his works. They are three novels, Frau Sorge *(Dame Care),* published in 1886, Der Katzensteg *(the name of a small wooden bridge over a waterfall that plays a prominent part in the story),* 1888, Es war *(It Was),* 1893; *three volumes of short tales,* Geschwister *(Brothers and Sisters), first published in the* Berliner Tageblatt *in* 1884 *and* 1886 *respectively (one of the stories,* Der Wunsch, *appears in the present volume),* Im Zwielicht *(In the Twilight), novelettes written in various newspapers, and* Iolanthe's Hochzeit *(Iolanthe's Wedding),* 1892; *and three dramas,* Die Ehre *(Honour),* Sodom's Ende *(The Destruction of Sodom), and* Heimat *(The Paternal Hearth).*

The most perfectly artistic of his longer novels, and that most deeply impregnated with the peculiar characteristics of East Prussian landscape is Frau Sorge. *Paul, the hero, is born just at the moment when his father's difficulties make it necessary for him to sell his house and land: this gloomy circumstance overshadows the whole of Paul's life. While his brothers and sisters in spite of the family poverty are, in their careless, unthinking way, happy and even prosperous, wilfully blind to the fact that they owe all to the industry and continual self-sacrifice of Paul, his life is one long toil and struggle, one long fidelity to duty as he conceives it, one long effacement and suppression of self. For this he receives no thanks, no acknowledgment. His spirit becomes crushed, almost extinguished. After long years of toiling, struggling, and suffering, he is redeemed through the love of a woman, but only when he has sacrificed to " Dame Care" all he held most precious, and when the capacity in him for joy and hope has been well-nigh destroyed. The character portrayed with perfect art is, at the same time, faithful to nature: such men are rare, perhaps, but it is well that the novelist should remind us of their existence, and thus help us to recognise the potency for good that dwells in mankind.*

Der Katzensteg *is more powerful but less artistic than* Frau Sorge. *The German critics, however, consider it to be not only the most important of Sudermann's writings, but the finest novel produced in Germany during this century. The character of the heroine, Regine, a veritable child of nature, in whom savagery and lack of intelligence and education exist side by side with the nobility and power of sacrifice, of which nature in the rough is often capable, forms the main interest of the tale, and is a marvellous and original conception. There is one scene that for realism, intensity, and horror has scarcely been surpassed in any novel of modern times.*

Before turning to the short tales in which we find some of Sudermann's best and most characteristic work, it would be well to point out one of his chief titles to genius. He has the gift of being able to describe terrible and heart-stirring scenes, joyful or pathetic or humorous scenes, with the utmost simplicity of style. In a few words of the simplest sort he brings before our eyes living pictures. Each sentence palpitates with life. As we read, we seem to live with the men and women of his creation through their agony ; we suffer as they do, and rejoice with them when they are glad: at times we are breathless as they are with suspense and excitement. And this is done without any of the analytical introspection with which we have become only too familiar in recent novels. The characters, at least in the novels and tales, are not mere nervous organisms, but living, loving, erring, feeling, human beings. The gift of terse narration joined to great simplicity of language is found in French writers like Flaubert and Maupassant, but it is new to Germany. It is, then, perhaps, Sudermann's highest praise that we can say of him that he possesses the strength without the unpleasantness of the great French writers of our day, and combines their artistic feeling, their power and their fine wit with all that is soundest and best in the Teutonic mind and character.

Many of the short tales are of a less specially German cast, and possess an interest that is universal. Der Wunsch (*The Wish*), *for instance, is a powerful psychological study, set forth with wonderful directness and simplicity. Although the tale deals with the old theme of a woman who falls in love with her sister's husband, it is instinct with passion and original in treatment. Olga loved her* sister Martha dearly, and had, indeed, brought about Martha's marriage with Robert Hellinger almost by her own efforts, but in so doing had herself, though unconsciously, fallen in love with Robert. Martha, always frail and delicate, after the birth of her child, falls dangerously ill. Olga goes to her to nurse her, and love for her sick sister and passion for Robert struggle for mastery in her soul. Thus, into a character entirely good, noble, and self-sacrificing, steals the wish, " if only she were to die!" In the event Martha does die. Then Robert's eyes are opened; he knows that he loves—has all along loved Olga, and he asks her to be his wife. At first she refuses, then consents; but the same night, having felt all the while that the wish for Martha's death, though never expressed by sign or word, makes her in a sense her sister's murderer, she puts an end to her life. She herself relates all the circumstances in a document written to explain her act to her old friend the physician. A couple of quotations will give a better idea of Sudermann's style than pages of criticism. In a few marvellous strokes he paints the effect on Robert of his first sight of Olga's corpse :—

" *When the elder Hellinger entered the room he saw a picture that froze the blood in his veins.*

" *His son's body lay stretched on the floor. In falling he must have clung to the posts of the bier on which they had placed the dead woman, thus bringing down the whole erection with him, for on top of him—among the broken boards—lay the corpse in its long white shroud, the stiffened face on his face, the bare arms thrown over his head."*

The scenes in Martha's sick room are portrayed with an art that makes them live in our memory. Here is one of them. Martha lies in bed sick unto death. Olga and Robert, wearied out with sleepless nights and with their terrible anxiety, are watching her.

" *There was absolute silence in the half-darkened room; only the wind with gentle rustling, swept past the window, and the mice scratched among the rafters of the ceiling.*

" *Robert buried his face in his hands and listened to Martha's dismal ravings. Gradually he seemed to grow calmer; his breathing became slower and more regular; now and again his head inclined to one side, but the next moment he drew it up again.*

" *Sleep overpowered him. I wanted to persuade him to go to bed but I was feared at the sound of my own voice and kept silent.*

" *The upper part of his body leaned over more and more frequently to one side ; at times his hair touched my cheek, and groping he sought a support.*

"*And then suddenly his head sank down on my shoulder and remained there.*

" *My body trembled as if an incredible happiness had befallen me. I was seized with an irresistible desire to stroke the bushy hair that fell over my face. Close to my eyes I saw a few silver threads. ' He is beginning to get grey,' I thought, ' it is high time that he should know what happiness means,' and then I actually stroked his hair.*

" *He sighed in his sleep and tried to place his head more comfortably.*

" ' *He is lying uncomfortably,' I said to myself, 'you must get close to him.' I did so. His shoulder lay against mine, and his head sank down on my bosom.*

" ' *You must put your arm round him,' something within me cried out, ' otherwise he cannot find rest.'*

" Twice, thrice, I tried to do so, but as often drew back.

" If Martha should suddenly wake ! But her eyes saw nothing, her ears heard nothing.

" And I did it.

" Then a wild joy took possession of me, and stealthily I pressed him to me ; something within me shouted joyously : ' Oh ! how I would cherish and protect you ; how I would kiss away the furrows misery has made in your brow, and the cares from your soul ! How I would toil for you with all my young strength, and never rest till your eyes were full of gladness, and your heart of sunshine. But to do that——'

" I glanced over at Martha. Yes, she lived, still lived. Her bosom rose and sank in short, quick sobs. She seemed more alive than ever.

" And suddenly there flamed before me, and it was as if I read written clearly on the wall the words :

" ' If only she were to die ! '

" ' Yes, that was it, that was it. Oh ! if only she were to die ! Oh ! if only she were to die ! '

We have only to read Jean Ricard's Sœurs, a novel lately published in Paris, and dealing with the same theme, to recognise how very far superior is Sudermann's treatment of it.

The volume of short tales entitled Im Zwielicht *is of a somewhat different character. Though coloured to some extent by the melancholy and "inevitableness" of the longer novels, those qualities are less intense, and we have lively touches of satire and brilliant flashes of wit that remind us of the sprightliness of French writers. The tales are told in the twilight by one or other of two friends, a man and a woman, between whom there exists merely an intellectual bond of sympathy and union. The stories laugh good-naturedly at narrow-mindedness and silly prejudice, an evil that Sudermann wisely recognises as existing everywhere, in the big city as in the small village. Women's social aspirations, their immense delight in entertaining celebrities, and their belief that in so doing they are moving in the stream of the world's history, are satirised with keenness and truth. He strikes a deeper note in the tale that sets forth the difficulties of friendship and love between a woman of mature years and a young man, a subject ably treated by Jean Richepin in his fine novel,* Madame André, *and it is very interesting to note the coincidence of view of the French and German writer. Perhaps Sudermann's views may help towards a satisfactory solution of that ever-recurring will-o'-the-wisp— platonic affection. His heroine declares that to turn friendship into love, or love into friendship, is impossible, because where such a transformation does take place, there must, in the first instance, have been either not friendship or not love. "From the day on which we reap love where we sowed friendship, the magic charm would be broken," she says. "Till then I was all and everything—then I should be merely one more." And again, "Love begins in the intoxication of the senses, and ends in the peace of calm friendship, that is, marriage; the contrary is not forbidden, but it leads—to the desert."*

In Iolanthe's Hochzeit, *Sudermann proves himself the possessor of the humour that borders on pathos. The little story has no tendency, it preaches no sermon. Onkel Hanckel, "a good fellow (*ein guter Kerl*) by profession," relates how he had to live up to the title, and how, at the mature age of forty-seven, he became, almost against his will,* *engaged to a young girl. His feelings at the wedding ceremony, his horror and shyness at the notion of being left alone with his bride afterwards, form a most delightful piece of comedy. Pütz, a surly, grasping, miserly, rich old man; Lothar, a dashing young lieutenant of dragoons; the maiden sister; and Iolanthe herself—are portrayed with a quaint humour of which the earlier works gave little indication, while the vigour, simplicity, and directness of the narrative are as fine as ever. The East Prussian dialect lends the original a local colour that would be difficult to reproduce in a translation.*

In his dramas Sudermann treats life very much from the same standpoint as Ibsen does. His characters talk a great deal, and do next to nothing. He wages war against shams, thinks people should live out their own lives and develop their individuality at all hazards. He presents abnormal types, men and women who would be abnormal anywhere, in civilised society or the reverse, and who must not be taken as representative of modern life. Each of the three dramas he has as yet given us presents a moral problem to the consideration of the spectators.

Die Ehre *was first performed at the Lessing Theatre in Berlin, on November 27, 1889, and had an immense success. The dramatist ruthlessly and boldly draws aside the curtain from the false ideas of honour held by high and low alike, not only by the middle class and proletariat of Berlin, but by civilised men in general: such social conventions, according to Sudermann, tend to make money-getting the sole aim of the citizen, and help to undermine the peace and happiness of family life. The revelation is undoubtedly unpleasing, but all the same a great truth underlies it, and in the end of the play the virtuous are not sacrificed to the wicked. In the speeches of Count Trast, the good angel, the god from the machine of the drama, it is not perhaps altogether fanciful to see the beliefs and opinions of Sudermann himself. Trast's conclusion is that we shall do better to substitute duty for the many and varied sorts of honour recognised by society.*

Sodom's Ende *is a startling play. Even the Berlin censorship required alterations before it could permit the production of the drama on the stage of the Lessing Theatre. It still contains one* scene that would effectually prevent its performance in an English playhouse. The drama takes its name from the title of a picture painted by Willy Janowski, who bids fair to become a great artist. But he has fallen under the influence of Adah Barcinowski, a cold, heartless, pleasure-loving woman, the wife of a wealthy stockbroker. That connection and his own weak nature have ruined Willy mentally, morally, and physically. He ceases to work, leads a life of self-indulgence, heedless of the hurt he does to others. The character, unpleasing as it is, is consistently drawn by the dramatist, for even in the pangs of death Willy does not cease to note the artistic pose taken by the dead body of the girl he has injured and betrayed. Never, perhaps, has the worst side of .h.it section of frivolous idle society we are accustomed to call "smart" been more ably painted: its foolish vapidity, its utter futility, and its elegant wickedness and sinfulness, are boldly displayed. Unfortunately men and women without conscience, without comprehension of duty, have always existed and still exist, but we doubt if their evil in-fluence is as far-reaching and all-important as latter-day novelists and dramatists would have us believe.

[*In his latest play*, Heimat, *produced January 7, 1893, Sudermann takes for theme the duty owed by the child to the parent, and that due from parent to child. A high-spirited and talented girl, daughter of commonplace, conventional parents, to the scandal of all concerned, leaves her home to carve for herself a career in the world, and by reason of her fine voice becomes a celebrated singer. After an absence of many years chance brings her professionally to her native town, and a very natural desire is awakened in her to revisit her parents and her home. Her father, whose health had been destroyed through the effects of her former disobedience, wishes her to come back provided she renounces for ever the life she has been leading. This she has no desire to do, but for her father's sake she is not all unwilling to yield. When, however, she is further required to break with certain ties very dear to her, she refuses, and the father dies from the shock. Now when we carefully read the play, or see it acted by competent artists, it is clear that much might be said on both sides. But as there is nothing in the world more beautiful and holy than the tie that binds parent* and child, so is the contemplation of conflict between them always unlovely. We grant that in the storm and stress of modern life such conflict is at times unavoidable, but it is scarcely the stuff of which works of art should be formed.⌋

A new play, a comedy, Schmetterling-Schlacht (Butterfly Battle), is to be produced shortly at the Hofburg Theatre in Vienna. Again a moral problem is to be presented to the consideration of the public. The three heroines, honest working girls, paint butterflies on fans for a living. Two of the girls, tired of being sweated, give up fan painting ; they take to painting their faces instead, and practice other abominations. The third girl continues her work, and remains virtuous. The play chiefly consists of a series of discussions between the girls as to which way of life is preferable.

Like his contemporaries, Ibsen and Björnson, Zola and Tolstoi, Sudermann would transfer the sermon from the pulpit to the stage : he sets before us certain phases of life that have come under his notice in all their ugliness and brutality, and would have us forthwith leave the theatre sworn enemies of the evils he denounces. But his characters are *contented to preach and discuss, they never feel that they are called upon to act. Thus they lack life and reality, we have little sympathy with them, and are never profoundly touched.*

As a writer of fiction, however, Sudermann's high position is unassailable. He ranks with the great masters in all countries who have sought, and are still seeking, to set before us modern life in its manifold aspects, in its complexity and its difficulties, but who, unlike the more pronounced school of naturalists, remember Joubert's maxim that "fiction has no business to exist unless it is more beautiful than reality."

August, 1894.

THE WISH.

In the old doctor's bedroom a cheerful fire was flickering. He himself still lay a-bed, quite penetrated by the delightful sensation of a man who knows his life's work is completed. When one has been sitting half a century through, for twelve long hours every day, in the rumbling conveyance of a country doctor, thumped and bumped along over stones and lumps of clay, one may now and again lie in bed till daylight, especially when one knows one's work is safe in younger hands.

He stretched and straightened his stiff old limbs, and once more buried in the pillows his weather-beaten, yellowish-grey face, covered with white stubble like granite with Iceland moss. But habit, that austere mistress, who had for so many years driven him forth from his bed before dawn, whether it was necessary or not, would not let him rest even now.

He sighed, he yawned, he abused his laziness, and then reached for the bell standing on the little table at his bedside.

His housekeeper, an equally grey, tumble-down specimen of humanity, appeared on the threshold.

"What time is it, Frau Liebetreu?" he called out to her.

Since the day on which the young assistant arrived in Gromowo, the old Black Forest clock hanging at the doctor's bedside, and whose rattling alarum had often unpleasantly jarred upon his morning slumbers, was no longer wound up. "So that I know that my life too henceforth stands still," as he was wont to say.

"A quarter to eight, doctor," the old woman answered, beginning meanwhile to busy herself about the stove.

"For shame! for shame!" cried he, raising himself up, "what a lazybones I am getting to be! I say, have any letters come?"

"Yes, a few by post, and one that young Mr. Hellinger brought himself two hours ago."

"Two hours ago! Why, it was dark yet at that time!"

"Yes; he said he had to drive out to the manor farm, and could wait no longer. Yesterday evening, too, when you were at the 'Black Eagle,' sir, he called, and sat here for about two hours."

"Why didn't you send for me?" cried the doctor, in the blustering tone of voice of old, good-natured grumblers.

"Well, and hadn't he forbidden us to do so?" cried his housekeeper, in exactly the same tone of voice, which seemed, however, more an echo of her master's manner than personal defiance. "He was sitting in the study till ten o'clock—or rather he was not sitting, he raced about like a madman, and laughed and talked to himself—I hardly knew the calm, quiet man again; and then I brought him beer—six bottles—he drained them all; and I had to drink with him. As I tell you, he was quite beside himself."

"Ah, indeed, indeed," muttered the old man

smiling to himself with satisfaction. "I should say Olga had something to do with that. Perhaps after all she——. Well, do you intend bringing me my letters to-day, or not?" he suddenly shouted, as if he were goodness knows how wild, but his face laughed the while. And when his housekeeper had grumblingly done his bidding, he drew out with a sure hand from the little heap of letters one without a stamp, not deigning to look at the others at all. His hands trembled with happy excitement as he unfolded the paper; and he read, while his grey face beamed with pleasure:

"DEAR OLD UNCLE,—You shall be the first to know it. If only I had you with me, that I might press your dear old hands and tell you face to face what is in my heart! I do not realise it yet—my head whirls when I think of it! Uncle, you were at my side in the days of darkest trouble, helping and protecting. You were the only one to take Martha's part when all — even my parents — turned their backs on her with coldness and suspicion.

"You could not save her for me, uncle—the Lord

asked her back of me. But when, at the bedside
of my dead wife, my reason threatened to give
way, you took my poor head between your hands
and spoke to me—as a preacher speaks. And you
were right. Of course I do not believe that I can
ever quite revive and become again as I was before
the cares of existence and my longing for Martha
made my head dull and heavy ; for even Martha—
even my wife—could not accomplish that in the
three years of our quiet happiness. But life seems
about to give me whatever it has left for me yet
of joy and peace. You know, uncle, how in the
midst of my sorrow for my dead wife, I learnt to
love her sister, Cousin Olga, more and more. I
confessed all to you, and sought comfort with you
when tortured by self-reproach at the thought
that I was breaking my troth to my wife already
in the year of mourning. And you said to me at
that time : ' If the dead woman might seek a
second mother for her child, whom else would she
choose but the sister whom, next to you, she loved
best in the world ? ' I was startled to the very
depths of my soul, for I should never have dared to
raise my eyes to her. But you never ceased to

encourage me, until, a week ago, I took heart and begged her to share my fortunes.

"You know she refused me.

"She grew deathly pale—then gave me her hand, and standing up rigidly said to me: 'Put it from your thoughts, Robert, for I can never be your wife.' Then I slunk away, and thought to myself, 'It serves you right for your presumption.' And now, to-day——. Uncle, I cannot put it on paper!—my hand fails me. This happiness is too great—it came so unexpectedly, it almost overpowers me! To-morrow, uncle—to-morrow I will tell you all.

"I have to go out early to the manor farm. At mid-day I shall return, and then forthwith shall undertake the dreaded visit to my parents. My mother suspects nothing as yet. Her plans have once again been frustrated, and Olga will have to suffer heavily enough for it. I fear she may even turn her out of the house. If only I had her already under my own roof!

"It is three o'clock in the morning. Enough for to-day. Your grateful and happy

"ROBERT HELLINGER."

The old doctor wiped a tear from his cheek.

"The dear boy," he murmured. "How his emotions crowd each other in his over-heated brain; and how simple, how honest everything is to the last jot! In truth, he deserves you, my brave, proud girl; he is the only one to whom I do not grudge you. And now I will put you to the test, and see if you too put confidence in your old uncle. Straightway I will do it."

Laughing and growling he burrowed with his head in the pillows. And then he suddenly shouted with a voice resounding through the house like thunder:

"Confound it, where are my trousers?"

The trousers were brought, and five minutes later the old man stood quite ready before his glass, all except his greyish-yellow wig.

"My hat, cloak, stick!" he shouted out into the corridor.

"But the breakfast," the old woman shouted back, if possible louder still, from the kitchen.

"Well, then, hurry up," he blustered. "Before I have read these letters I must have it here."

With an impatient oath he set to work upon the

little heap that had so far been lying unnoticed on the pedestal. Offers of wine—profitable investments—a poor, blind father with a new-born infant—and then suddenly he stopped short, while once more a satisfied smile overspread his features.

" Upon my word ! I should not have expected this," he growled, contentedly. " She, too, could not rest without confiding her happiness to her old uncle. That is nice of you, children ! You shall have your reward for this."

With the same happy haste with which he had opened Hellinger's letter, he tore this envelope asunder.

But hardly had he commenced reading when with a low moaning cry he staggered back two paces, like one who has been dealt a treacherous blow. His grey face became ashy pale ; his eyes started from their sockets, and like claws his old withered fingers clutched the fluttering paper.

When his housekeeper brought in the coffee, she found her master sitting as stiff as a log in the corner of the sofa, his forehead covered with great drops of perspiration, and staring with fixed lustreless eyes at the paper which his hands still held as if in a cramp.

"Gracious heavens, doctor!" she cried, and let the tray drop clattering on to the table. Her lamentations brought him back to consciousness. He asked for water, and drank two long eager draughts, wetted his forehead and temples with the remainder, and signed to his housekeeper to leave him.

Hereupon he bolted the door, picked up the letter from the floor, and read with trembling, choking voice:

"MY DEAR, MY FATHERLY FRIEND,—When you read these lines I shall have ceased to live. The draughts of morphium which you gave me when I had forgotten how to sleep after Martha's death were carefully collected and kept by me; I trust they will be powerful enough to give me peace.

"You who have watched over me like a second father, you shall be the only one to learn why I have decided to take this terrible step. In long winter nights, when the storm shook my gable-roof and I could not sleep, I wrote down everything that has been tormenting me for so long, and will not let me be at rest till I fall asleep for ever. On my bookshelf, hidden behind some volumes of Heine, you will find a blue exercise-book. Take it with you, without letting the others notice. And when you have read all, go out to my grave and there say a prayer for my soul.

" See that I am laid to rest at Martha's side.

" I loved her dearly. It is she who is calling me to her.

" You will understand all when you have read my story. Perhaps you know more of my secret than I suspect. I suppose I must have spoken evil words during the delirium of my illness, else why should you have sent away my relations from my bedside ?

" Did you shudder at the things that my wretched tongue brought to light ?

" Do you pity me ? Do you despise me ? No, surely you do not despise me ; or how could you have bestowed so much love upon me ? And now read. Everything is set down there. It was not originally intended for you. I meant to send it after many years—when we young ones too should have grown old—to the man to whom my whole being belongs, so that he might know why I once denied myself to him.

"Things have gone differently. To-day, in a moment of forgetfulness, I threw myself upon his neck. Too late I comprehended that now escape from him was no longer possible. But, rather than be his, I will seek death.

"And I have yet another request in my heart. It is the request of one about to die—if you can, I know you will fulfil it.

"Keep secret from the world, and especially from the man I love, that I took my own life. Let him believe that my happiness killed me. I shall destroy everything that might point to suicide; there will only be indications that I died of syncope or apoplexy.

"From the depths of my heart I implore you to grant me this one last favour. I die gladly and have no fear. It is so long since I slept well, that I have need of rest.   "OLGA BREMER."

The old man felt himself in a state of utter helplessness.

He staggered, clenched his fists, beat his brow, and then once more he fell back in his chair.

"This is madness, utter madness," he groaned, wiping the cold perspiration from his forehead. "Child, what were you thinking of? What could cloud your reason like this? My poor, poor, darling child?"

Then he once more jumped up and groped with trembling fingers for his hat and cloak.

"To help! To help!" He must wrest this victim even yet from death's hand! That was what absorbed his whole mind at present. For a moment the thought came to him that perhaps after all she had not carried out her serious intention, but he dismissed it forthwith. He must have had a different knowledge of her character, to credit her with a feeling of fear or a failing of energy.

But possibly the dose she had taken was too small, perhaps the long period of time—for it was more than a year since Martha died in child-bed, and it was then he had given her the sleeping draughts—perhaps the long period of time that had elapsed since then had weakened the efficacy

of the poison.   Yes, yes, it was so ; it must be so !
When badly preserved, morphia decomposes and
becomes ineffectual.

So forward to the rescue !   To save what can be
saved !

He ran about the room in search of something :
he hardly knew what he was seeking.   Then once
more he grasped the letter.

" And what do you ask of me ?   Child, child, do
you think it is such a light matter to perjure one's
self?   To throw aside like rotten eggs the duties
to which one has been faithful for half a century ?
Child, you do not realise what you are asking of
an honest man ! "   He held the paper up close to
his eyes, and once more read the passage : " It is
the request of one about to die. . . . From the
depths of my heart I implore you to grant me this
one last favour."

Heavy tears rolled down his weather-beaten
cheeks.

" It cannot be, child, it cannot be done, however
well you may know how to plead.   And even if I
wished to do it, I should betray myself.   I am an
old, weak wreck ; I no longer have such control

over my features. They would notice it at the first glance. But so that you may not have asked it—of your old uncle—in vain—I will—at least attempt it—for your own sake and Robert's sake you must first of all be saved. Confound it all, old fellow, for once more in your life be a man— you must save her—you must—must—must!"

And as quickly as his stiff old legs would carry him, he rushed out—past his housekeeper, who stood listening at the keyhole—out into the wintry morning air which a cold drizzling mist filled with damp, prickling crystals.

II.

A very picture of perfect serenity and peace of mind the couple Hellinger senr. made, as they sat at the breakfast-table. Out of the spout of the brass coffee-machine on the brightly-polished body of which the fire-flames produced a purple reflection, there rose up thin, bluish steam which sank down towards the table in little clouds, cast a film over the silver sugar-basin and wreathed the coffee-cups with delicate, tiny dewdrops.

Mr. Hellinger, with his snow-white, carefully trimmed beard, and handsome, rosy, boyish face beaming with good nature and the pleasure of living, was leaning back comfortably in the blue chintz armchair, his Turkish dressing-gown pulled over his knees, and apparently awaiting with calmest resignation whatever fate, in the shape of his wife, might be about to bestow upon him.

She (his wife) was just throwing a pinch of soda

into the little coffee-pot, whereupon she circumstantially wiped her powdery fingers on her white damask apron, which was edged in Russian fashion with broad red and many coloured stripes. Her white matron's cap, the ribbons of which were tightly knotted together like a chin strap under her fleshy chin, had shifted somewhat towards the left ear, and from out its frilly frame there shone, full of energy and enterprise, her coarse, comfortable, sergeant-like face, whose features were rather puffed out, as is often observable in old women who like to share their husband's glass of brandy.

One could see that she was accustomed to rule and to subdue, and even the smile of constant injured feeling that played about her broad mouth went to prove how inconsiderately she was wont to carry through her plans.

So that she might not sit unoccupied while waiting for the coffee to draw, she took up her coarse woollen knitting, which, in her capacity of president of the ladies' society and directress of the charity organisation, was never allowed to leave her hands, and the needles ran with remarkable rapidity through her bony, work-used fingers.

"Have you heard nothing from Robert, Adalbert?" she asked, with a hard metallic voice, which must have penetrated the house to its last corner.

The question appeared to be unpleasant to the old man. He shook his head as if he would shake it off; it disturbed his morning tranquillity.

"An affectionate son, one must say," she continued, and the injured smile grew in intensity. "Since a week we have neither heard nor seen anything of him ; if he lived in the moon he could not come more rarely."

Mr. Hellinger muttered something to himself, and busied himself with his long pipe.

"It looks as if something were brewing again in that quarter," she began anew ; "he has altogether been so peculiar lately ; come slinking round me without a word to say for himself. It seems to me there is some debt hanging over him again that he can't satisfy."

"Poor fellow," said the old man, and smacked his lips, perhaps to get rid of the unpleasant idea by this means.

"Poor fellow, indeed !" she mocked him ; "I

suppose you pity him into the bargain ; perhaps even you have been helping him on the sly ? "

He raised up his white, well-kept hands in protest and defence of himself, but he had not the courage to look her in the face.

"Adalbert," she said, threateningly, "I make it a condition that such a thing does not happen again. Whatever you give him, you take from us and from our other children. And if at least he deserved it ! but he that will not hear advice must suffer. If he is ruined, with his obstinacy and stubbornness——"

"Allow me, Henrietta," he interrupted her timidly.

"I allow nothing, Adalbert, my dear," replied she. "' He that will not hearken to advice must suffer !' say I ; and if through his abominable ingratitude his poor mother, who is only anxious for his welfare, and who bothers and worries herself whole nights through, thinking——"

With the many-coloured border of her apron she rubbed her eyes as if there were tears there to be wiped away.

"But, Henrietta," he began again.

" Adalbert, do not contradict me! You know I close an eye to all your follies. I allow you to sit as long as ever you like at the ' Black Eagle '; I let you drink as much as ever you can do with of that bad, expensive claret. I even put your supper ready for you when you come home late though it is hardly necessary that you should on such occasions upset three chairs, as you did yesterday. I consider altogether that you have very little regard for the feelings of your old and faithful wife. But—yes, what I was going to say is—that, once for all, I will not have you meddle with my plans: as it is you understand nothing of such matters. Have you, altogether, any idea of all I have done already for that good-for-nothing Robert ? I have run about, and driven about, made calls, and written letters, and Heaven knows what else. Five or six well-to-do—nay, very wealthy girls I have, so to say, brought ready to his hand, any of whom he could have had for the taking. But what did he do ? Well, I should think you still remember how I was seized with convulsions when, four years ago, he arrived with that miserable, delicate creature, Martha? My whole illness dates from then."

"But, Henrietta!"

"My dear Adalbert, I beg of you, do not again harp upon the same old string about her being my own flesh and blood! If she wished to be a loving and grateful niece to me, why did she not bring the necessary dowry with her? She had nothing —of course she had nothing! My departed brother died as poor as a church mouse. Is that fitting for one of my family? But after all—he had a right to do as he liked with his own—what business is it of mine? Only he need not have saddled us with his daughter."

"Well, but she is dead now," remarked Herr Hellinger.

"Yes, she is dead," replied she, and folded her hands. "It were a sin to say, thank God for that. But as our Lord has so ordained it, I will at least profit by the circumstance, and endeavour to rectify his folly of then. While you were sitting in the 'Black Eagle,' drinking your claret, I was once more toiling and moiling and inquiring round, so that he has but to pick and choose. There is

Gertrude Leuzmann ; will get fifty thousand cash down and as much more when the old man dies. There is that little von Versen ; very young yet certainly—only just confirmed—but she will get even more ! And besides these, at least three or four others ! But what do you imagine he will say to it all ? ' Mother,' he will say, ' if you start that theme again, you will never more set sight on me.' Was ever such a thing heard of? He has only to marry the second sister now in place of the other one, to bring his good old mother to her grave ! By the by where can the young lady be to-day ? It is nearly nine o'clock, and she has not yet appeared. In my brother's Bohemian home it may very probably have been the fashion to lie a-bed till noon ; but in my well-ordered household, I beg to say, most emphatically and politely, I will not have it, Adalbert."

"I cannot conceive, dear Henrietta," he said, "why you heap reproaches upon me which are meant for your niece ! "

"If only for once you would not take her part, Adalbert. But, of course, there is nothing left for me to say. I am duped and betrayed in my own house!   However, I shall very soon put an end to the matter.   I have kept her here now for a whole year; now she begins to be very much *de trop*."

"But does she not toil and moil in Robert's household from early morn till late at night? Does a day pass on which she does not betake herself to the manor farm? Do not be unjust towards her, Henrietta."

She gave him a pitying look.

"If you had not remained such a child, Adalbert, one might talk reason to you. Don't you see that that is just where the danger lies? Don't you imagine that she has her reasons for flaunting about every day at the manor and for behaving herself as mistress there before him and the servants? Ah—she—she is a deep one—is my niece Olga. Be sure she has done her part towards getting him accustomed to the idea that she—and she alone—has a right to the place of her dead sister. What else should she be looking for, day after day, at the manor, if it is not that?"

"I should think Martha's child is sufficient explanation."

"Of course, of course! Any nursery tale is good enough to impose upon you! She knows exactly why she behaves as she does, and why she is almost ready to eat up the poor little mite for very love. She knows exactly how to find the way to its father's heart!"

"But perhaps she does not love him at all," old Hellinger interposed.

She laughed out loud.

"My dear Adalbert, a man who owns an estate just outside the town-gates is always loved by a poor girl, and if I do not make an end now and send her about her business, it may very possibly come to pass that our dear Robert will take her by the hand one fine day and say to us, 'Here, papa and mamma, now be good enough to give us your blessing.' And rather than live to see that, Adalbert——"

At this moment the sound of lumbering male steps was audible in the entrance-hall; directly after these came a loud and violent knock at the door.

"Well!" said Mrs. Hellinger, "some one is making a noise as if the bailiffs were outside—

we have not got as far as that yet." And very slowly and deliberately she said, "Come in."

The old doctor stepped into the room. His hat sat awry at the back of his head, his necktie hung loose over his shoulders, and his chest heaved as with breathless running. He forgot his "Good-morning" greeting, and only gave a wild, searching glance around.

"Good heavens, doctor!" cried Mr. Hellinger, sen., hastening towards him, "why, you burst in upon us like a bull into a china-shop."

Mrs. Hellinger once more assumed her injured air, and muttered something about pot-house manners.

When the old doctor saw the undisturbed breakfast-table and the astonished, every-day faces of his friends, he let himself drop into an armchair with a sigh of relief. Then it had not taken place after all—this terrible thing! But next moment his fears took possession of him anew.

"Where is Olga?" he faltered, and fixed his gaze on the door as if he might see her enter there any moment.

"Olga?" said Mrs. Hellinger, shrugging her

shoulders. "My goodness, she probably will be here shortly. Are you in such a hurry?"

"God be praised!" cried he, folding his hands. "Then she has been down already?"

"No—not so," remarked Mrs. Hellinger, "her ladyship thinks well to sleep somewhat long this morning."

"For God's sake," he cried, "has no one looked after her? Does no one know anything of her?"

"Doctor, what ails you?" cried old Hellinger, who was now beginning to be alarmed.

The physician may at this moment have recollected the request with which Olga's letter of farewell had closed. He felt that in this way his desire to comply with her request would, from the very first, become impossible, and made a last wretched attempt to preserve the secret.

"What ails me?" he faltered, with a miserable laugh. "Nothing ails me!—What should ail me? Confound it all!" And then, casting aside all dissimulation, he cried out: "My God! my God! Thou hast permitted this terrible thing! Thou hast withdrawn Thy hand from her." And he was about to sink down weeping, but he once more gathered up all the energy still remaining in his rickety old body, raised himself bolt upright, and—"Come to Olga," he said, "and do not be terrified—however—you may—find her."

Old Hellinger grew pale, and his wife commenced to scream and sob; she clung to the doctor's arm, and wished to know what had happened; but he spoke no further word.

So they all three climbed up the stairs leading to Olga's gable-room, and in the entrance-hall the servants collected and stared after them with great, inquisitive eyes.

Before Olga's door Mrs. Hellinger was seized with a paroxysm of despair.

"You knock, doctor," she sobbed, "I cannot."

The old man knocked.

All remained quiet.

He knocked again, and put his ear to the keyhole.

As before.

Then Mrs. Hellinger began to scream:

"Olga, my beloved, my dear child, do open— we are here—your uncle and aunt and old uncle doctor are here. You may open without fear, my love."

The physician pressed the latch ; the door was locked. He looked through the key-hole ; it was stopped up.

" Have the locksmith fetched, Adalbert," he said.

" No," cried Mrs. Hellinger, suddenly casting all sorrow to the winds, " that I shall not permit— that will on no account be done. The disgrace would be too great: I could never survive it— such a disgrace—such a disgrace ! "

The doctor gave her a look of unmistakable loathing and contempt. She took little notice of it.

" You are strong, Hellinger," she said, " bear up against the door; perhaps you may succeed in breaking the lock."

Mr. Hellinger was a giant. He set one of his powerful shoulders against the woodwork, which at the first pressure began to crack in its joints.

" But softly," his wife admonished, " the servants are standing in the entrance-hall. Be off with you into the kitchen, you lazy beggars ! " she shouted scolding down the stairs.

Down below doors banged. A second push—

one of the boards broke right through the middle. Through the splintry chink a bright ray of day-light broke through into the semi-dark corridor.

"Let me look through," said the doctor, who now, in anticipation of the worst, was calm and collected.

Hellinger broke off a few splinters, so that through the aperture the whole room could be overlooked.

Opposite the door, a few paces removed from the window, stood the bed. The coverlet was dragged up, and formed a white hillock behind which a strip of Olga's light brown hair shone forth. A small portion of the forehead was also visible—white as the bed-clothes it gleamed. The feet were uncovered ; they seemed to have been firmly set against the foot end of the bed and then to have relaxed.

By the pillow, on a chair, lay her clothes neatly folded. Her skirts, her stockings, were laid one upon the other in perfect symmetry, and on the carpet stood her slippers, with their heels turned towards the bed, so as to be quite ready for slipping into on rising.

On the marble slab of the pedestal, half leaning against the lamp, lay a book, still open, as if it had been placed there before extinguishing the light. Over everything there seemed to rest a shimmer of that serene, unconscious peace which irradiates a pure maiden's soul. She who dwelt here had fallen asleep yesterday with a prayer on her lips, to awaken to-day with a smile.

After the physician had held silent survey, he stepped back from the aperture.

"Put your arm through, Adalbert," he said, "and try to reach the lock. She has bolted the door from the inside."

But Mrs. Hellinger squeezed herself up against the door, and with loud cries implored her sweet one to wake up and draw the bolt herself. At last it was possible to push her on one side, and the door was opened. The three stepped up to the bedside.

A marble-white countenance, with lustreless, half-open eyes, and an ecstatic smile on its lips, met their gaze. The beautiful head, with its classic, refined features, was slightly bowed towards the left shoulder, and the unbound hair fell down in great shining waves upon the regal bust, over which the nightdress was torn. A white button with a shred of linen attached, which hung in the buttonhole, was the only sign that a state of excitement must have preceded slumber.

"My sweet one, you are sleeping, are you not?" sobbed Mrs. Hellinger. "Say that you are sleeping! You cannot have brought such disgrace upon your aunt, your dear aunt, who cared for you and watched over you like her own child." With that she seized the unconscious girl's pale, pendant, white hand, and endeavoured to drag her up by it.

Her tender-hearted husband had covered his face with his hands, and was weeping. The physician gave himself no time for emotion. He had pulled out his instruments, pushed Mrs. Hellinger aside with scant politeness, and was bending over the bosom, which with one rapid touch he entirely freed of its covering.

When he rose up, every drop of blood had left his face.

"One last attempt," he said, and made a quick incision straight across the upper arm, where an artery wound itself in a bluish line through the white, gleaming flesh. The edges of the wound gaped open without filling with blood ; only after some seconds a few sluggish, dark drops oozed forth.

Then the old man threw the shining little knife far from him, folded his hands and—struggling with his tears—uttered a prayer.

III.

ON the afternoon of the same day, a light one-horse cabriolet sped over the common which extends across country for several miles northwards of Gromowo, and in the direction of the little town.

Dark and lowering, as if within reach of one's hand, the clouds lay over the level plain. Here and there a willow stump stretched its gnarled excrescences into the fog-laden air, all saturated with moisture and glistening with the drops which hung in long rows on its bare branches. The wheels sank deep into the boggy road, winding along between withered reed-grass, and often the water splashed up as high as the box-seat.

The man who held the reins took little heed of the surrounding landscape; quite lost in thought he sat huddled up, only occasionally starting up when the reins threatened to slip from his careless fingers. Then the herculean build of his limbs became apparent, and his broad, high-arched chest expanded as if it would burst the coarse grey cloak which stretched across it in scanty folds.

The man's stature was similar to that of old Hellinger, perhaps even superior, and the face, too, bore an undeniable family resemblance ; but what had there remained pleasing and soft and undefined even in old age, had here developed into harsh, impressive lines, testifying to defiance and gloomy brooding. A curly, terribly-neglected beard in dark disorder encompassed the firm-set jaw, assumed a lighter dye near the corners of the mouth, and fell upon the breast in two fair points.

This was Robert Hellinger, the owner of Gromowo manor, Olga's betrothed. Of the happiness that had come to him yesterday there was little written in his face. His grey, half-veiled eyes stared moodily into the distance, and the wrinkles between his eyebrows never for one moment disappeared. He well knew that hard work was in store for him before he could lead home his bride —hours of bitterest struggle were imminent, and even victory would bring him nothing but care and anxiety. His thoughts travelled back over the dark times that lay in the past, and that had hardly ever been illumined by a ray of light.

It was now six years since his father had solemnly made over to him, as eldest son, the old family inheritance, the manor, and had himself retired to a comfortable quiet life in the little town. On this day his period of suffering had commenced, for he was burdened with a yoke so heavy that even his herculean shoulders threatened to break under its weight ; everything he gained by the work of his sinewy hands—everything of which he positively pinched himself—melted away and was swallowed up by the claims which his family laid upon him. He had no right to complain. Was it not all according to strict law ? The inheritance had been exactly divided to the very last farthing among him and his six brothers and sisters, not counting the reserve which his parents claimed for themselves.

Every brick of his house, every clod of his land, was encumbered—on every ear of corn ripening in his fields his mother's suspicious gaze was fixed, for she kept strict watch lest the interests should come in a minute late. And was she not justified in so doing? Had he a right to claim more love from her than she gave to her other children? There were brothers who wanted to make their way in the world ; sisters who had only been married for the sake of their dowry : they all looked anxiously and eagerly towards him as the promoter and preserver of their happiness.

The interests! That was the dreadful word that henceforth hour by hour droned in his ears, that by night startled him from his sleep and filled his dreams with wild visions. The interests! How often on their account he had beaten his brow with clenched fists! How often he had run without sense or feeling through the loamy fields, to escape from this host of glinting, gleaming devils! How often in a blind fit of rage he had smashed to pieces some tool, a ploughshare, a waggon-pole, with his fist, as if he did not mind with what weapon he fought them! But they did not leave him. All the more tenaciously did they fasten themselves on to his heels; all the more thirstily did they suck the marrow from his young bones.

What good was it that he sometimes succeeded in mastering them ? This hydra everlastingly brought forth new heads ; from quarter to quarter it stood there before his terrified gaze, more and more monstrous, more and more gigantic, growing and swelling, ready to pounce upon him and crush him with the weight of its body. Thus from one reprieve to the next his life had dragged along since that day which was so merrily celebrated at the "Black Eagle" with drinking of claret and champagne.

If only his mother had exercised some leniency ! But she did not even exempt him from the stipulated asparagus in spring, nor even from the loan of the carriage for drives during harvest-time when the horses were so badly wanted in the fields.

"He that will not hearken to advice must suffer," she was wont to say, and he would not hearken ; no, indeed not ! With one short, simple "yes" he might have put a stop to all his misery, might have lived in the lap of luxury to the end of his days ; and because he would not do it, out of sheer, inconceivable stubbornness, because all her wife-hunting had been to no purpose—that was why his mother could not forgive him.

Thus two years passed away. Then he began to feel that such a life must sooner or later make a wreck of him. This anxiety and worry was exhausting him more and more ; he decided to put an end to it all and to demand of fate that modest share of happiness which was pledged and promised to him by a pair of faithful blue eyes, and a pale, gentle mouth. Then came a day when he brought home, as wife to his hearth, the love of his youth, who had shortly become orphaned and homeless.

It was a dreary, sad November day, and dark clouds sped like birds of ill omen across the sky. Trembling and pale, in her black mourning dress, the frail, delicate creature hung on his arm and quaked beneath every half-compassionate, half-contemptuous glance with which the strange people examined her.

As for his mother, she had received her with reproaches and maledictions, and a year had elapsed before tolerable relations were established between the two.

Martha had kept up bravely, and in spite of her

delicate health, had worked from morn to night in order to set to rights what had all gone topsy-turvy during the master's long bachelorhood.

And when, after three years of quiet, cheering companionship, Heaven was about to bless their union, she had—even when her condition already required the greatest care—always been up and doing, working and ordering in kitchen, attic, and cellar.

It almost seemed as if thus by labour she wanted to give an equivalent for her missing dowry.

Then—two days after the birth of a child—Olga had suddenly arrived in Gromowo. He had not seen her since his marriage. At first sight of her he was almost startled. She came towards him with an expression of such proud reserve and bitterness; she had blossomed forth to such regal beauty.

And this woman he was to-day to call his own! Yet what a world of suffering, how many days of gloomiest brooding and despair, how many nights full of horrible visions lay between now and then!

He shuddered ; he did not like to recall it any more. To-day everything seemed to have turned out well ; Martha's glorified image smiled down in peace and benediction, and, like a flower sprung from her grave, happiness was blooming anew for him.

Nearer and nearer came the turrets of the little town ; higher and higher they stretched up behind the alder thickets. And a quarter of an hour later the carriage drove into the roughly-paved street.

Soon after entering the gates Robert made the discovery that people who met him to-day behaved towards him in the most peculiar manner. Some avoided him, others in evident confusion doffed their caps and then as quickly as possible fled from his presence. On the other hand, the windows of every house past which the carriage drove, filled with heads that stared at him gravely and disappeared hurriedly behind the curtains at his greeting.

He shook his head doubtfully. But as his mind was so full of the approaching struggle, he took not much notice, and henceforth looked neither to the right nor to the left. At the corner of the market-place, where there used to be the little excise-office, stood his uncle's, the doctor's, old housekeeper, holding her hands hidden under her blue apron, and with an expression on her face like that of an undertaker.

As the carriage approached, she signed to him to stop.

"Well, Mrs. Liebetreu," he said, amused, "you at least do not take to your heels at my approach to-day."

The old woman gazed up at the sky, so that she might not have to look him in the face.

"Oh! young master," said she—he was always called "young master," to distinguish him from his father, though he was long past thirty—"the doctor wishes me to ask if you will kindly just step round there first; he has something to say to you."

"Is what he has to say to me very pressing?"

The woman was very much terrified, for she thought the unhappy intelligence would now fall to her lot to tell.

"Oh, gracious me!" she said; "he only put it like that."

"Well, then, give my kindest regards to my uncle the doctor, and the message, that I only just wanted first to have a little talk with my parents—

he knows what about—and will then come round to him at once."

The old woman muttered something, but the words stuck in her throat. The carriage rolled on in the direction of old Hellinger's villa, that lay there under mighty old lime-trees, as if resting beneath a canopy. The bright plate-glass windows greeted him cheerily, the shining tiled roof gleamed in the light, the tranquillity of a well-provisioned old age rested, as usual, over all. He tied his horse to the garden-railings, and strode with heavy, noisy tread up the small flight of steps, on the parapet of which, in wide-bellied urns, half-faded aster plants mournfully drooped their heads.

The hall-bell sounded in shrill tones through the house, but no one put in an appearance to receive him. He threw down his rain-soaked cloak on one of the oak chests in which his mother's linen treasures were hidden away. Then he stepped into the sitting-room—it was empty.

" The old people are probably taking their afternoon nap," he muttered ; "and I think it will be advisable to let them have their sleep out to-day."

He flung himself into a corner of the sofa, and gazed towards the door; for he privately hoped that Olga might have noticed his conveyance in front of the house, and would come down to shake hands with him.

He began to get impatient. "Can she have gone out to the manor?" he asked himself. But, no—she would not do that; for she knew he would come to speak to his parents.

"I will knock at her door," he decided, and got up.

He smiled anxiously, and stretched his mighty limbs. After having longed for her incessantly since yesterday evening, now, at the moment of beholding her again, he was filled with a peculiar fear of facing her. The feeling of humble reverence, which always took possession of him in her presence, now again made itself evident. Was it possible that this woman had yesterday hung upon his neck? And what if she regretted it to-day—if she went back from her word?

But at this moment all his defiance awoke within him. He opened his arms wide, and with a smile which reflected the memory of happy hours recently lived through, he cried :

"Let her but dare such a thing! With these hands of mine I will lift her up and carry her to my home! If Martha gives her consent, I wonder who should object."

On tip-toe, so as not to wake his parents, he climbed up the stairs, which nevertheless creaked and groaned under the weight of his body.

Before Olga's door he started back, for he saw the gleam of light which fell through the broken panel on to the corridor.

No one answered to his knocking. Nevertheless, he entered.

*　　*　　*　　*　　*

A moment later the whole house trembled in its foundations, as if the roof had fallen in.

The two old people, who had retired to their bedroom to recuperate their strength after those trying hours of the forenoon, started up in terror. They called the maids. But these had run off, so that the town should no longer be kept in ignorance of the newest details about the sad occurrence.

"You go up," said the energetic woman to her husband, and tremblingly put out her hand for the little bottle of sulphuric ether which she always kept at hand. It was the first time in her life that she felt frightened.

When old Hellinger entered the gable-room, he saw a sight which froze the blood in his veins.

His son's body lay stretched on the ground. As he fell he must have clutched the supports of the bier on which the dead girl had been placed, and dragged down the whole erection with him ; for on the top of him, between the broken planks, lay the corpse, in its long white shroud, its motionless face upon his face, its bared arms thrown over his head.

At this moment he regained consciousness, and started up. The dead girl's head sank down from his, and bumped on to the floor.

"Robert, my boy !" cried the old man, and rushed towards him.

With wide-open, glassy eyes, Robert stared about him. He seemed not yet to have recovered his senses. Then he perceived one of the arms, which, as the body dropped sidewards, had fallen right across his chest. His gaze travelled along it up to the shoulder, as far as the neck—as far as the white rigidly-smiling face.

Supported by the old man's two arms, he raised himself up. He tottered on his legs like a bull that has received a blow from an axe.

"Good God, boy, do come to your senses!" cried his father, taking him by his shoulders. "The misfortune has taken place; we are men, we must keep our composure."

His son looked at him vacantly, helplessly as a child. Then he bent over the dead body, lifted it up, and laid it across the bed, pushing the fragments of the bier to one side with his foot.

Then he seated himself close to her on the pillow, and mechanically wound a coil of her flowing hair round his finger.

The old man began to entertain fears of his son's sanity.

"Robert," he said, coming close up to him again, "pull yourself together. Come away from here; you cannot bring her back to life again."

Then he broke into a laugh so shrill and horrible, that it froze the very marrow in his father's bones.

All of a sudden his stupor left him ; he jumped up, his eyes glowed, and on his temples the veins swelled up.

"Where is mother?" he screamed, advancing towards the old man.

He sought to pacify him.

"Good heavens! do have patience! We will tell you all."

The old lady, who had already been standing for a long time listening on the stairs, at this moment put in her head at the door.

He rushed past his father and at her as if about to strangle her; but he had at least so much reason left as to be sensible of the monstrousness of his proceeding. His arms fell down limp at his sides—he set his teeth as if to choke down his pent-up rage. "Mother," said he, "you shall account to me for this. I demand an explanation of you. Why did she die?"

The old woman came towards him with tender compassion, and made as if she would burst into tears upon his neck.

With a rough movement he shook her off.

"Leave that, mother" he said, "I claim her from you!"

"But, Robert," whined the old woman, "is this the way for a son to treat his mother! Adalbert, just tell him how he ought to treat his mother!"

He took hold of the old man's hands. "You keep out of the game, father," he said. "The account which I have to settle to-day with my mother concerns us two alone. Mother, I ask you once more: why did she die?" He was leaning against the wall and stared at her with half-closed, blood-shot eyes.

Mrs. Hellinger had meanwhile commenced to cry.

"Do you suppose I know?" she sobbed; "do you suppose anybody at all knows? We found her in her bed, that is all. She has brought disgrace upon our house, the miserable creature, in return for——"

"Do not abuse her, mother," he said, wildly, speaking in an angry undertone; "you know very well that she was my bride!"

His mother gave vent to a cry of astonishment, and her husband too made a movement of surprise.

"What! you do not know that? Mother," he cried, and pressed both his fists to his temples, "did she say nothing to you? Did she not come to you last night, and tell you what had taken place between her and me during the day?"

"Heaven forbid!" groaned the old woman. "Scarce a syllable did she speak to me, but went and locked herself up in her room."

"Mother," he said, and stepped close up to her. "When she had confessed all to you, did you not work upon her conscience? Did you not impress it upon her that if she truly loved me she must give me up, that she would bring misfortune upon me, and Heaven knows what besides! Mother, did you not do this?"

"My own son does not believe me! My own son gives me the lie," whimpered the old woman. "These are the thanks that I get from my children to-day."

He grasped her right hand. "Mother," he said, "you have done me many a wrong in all these years. The worst and bitterest I ever experienced came to me through you."

" Merciful Heavens," shrieked the old woman, " these are the thanks—these are the thanks ! "

"But all the evil you did to me and Martha I will forgive you, mother," he continued, "nay, more even ! On my bended knees I will ask your forgiveness for ever having harboured a bitter thought against you ; but one thing you must do for me—here by her dead body you must swear that you knew of nothing, that in all things you were speaking the truth." And he dragged her to the corpse that stared up at him with its ecstatic smile—a bride's smile to her bridegroom.

" That such a thing should be necessary between us," complained the old woman, and cast a glance of bitter hatred at him out of her swollen eyes. But she suffered him to lay her right hand on the dead girl's forehead ; she stroked it and sobbed, " I swear it, my sweet one, you know best that I knew nothing and never required anything wrong of you." Thereupon she gave a sigh of relief, as if she had suddenly come to understand what a gain this tragic deed would mean for her and her family. Sincere gratitude lay in the tender caress with which she fondled the dead face.

At this moment the old physician came rushing into the room. He had hoped to overtake Robert and prepare him for the worst, and saw in terror that he had come too late.

Old Hellinger hurried towards him and whispered in his ear: "Take him away, he is out of his senses! We can do nothing with him here!"

Robert stood there clutching at the bed-posts, his chest heaving, his face as if turned to stone with gloomy, tearless misery.

The old doctor rubbed his stubbly grey beard against his shoulder, and growled in that roughly compassionate way which goes quickest to the hearts of strong men.

"Come away, my boy; don't do anything foolish; do not disturb her rest."

Robert started and nodded several times.

Then suddenly — as if overpowered by his misery—he fell down in front of the bed and cried out, "Wherefore didst thou die?"

IV.

Wherefore had she died ?

This question henceforth puzzled the whole town completely. In the streets—at the tea-table, on the alehouse benches—it was the one topic for discussion. People indulged in the most out-of-the-way surmises, the most hazardous con-jectures were put forward, and still no one was one whit the wiser. Some spoke of an unhappy, others of an over-happy love affair, and others again declared that they had always predicted that she would not come to a good end.

During her life-time already, her proud, taciturn, reserved nature had been a riddle to the good homely townfolk ; now her death was a still greater riddle to them.

Meanwhile it had got about that the physician had been the first to receive news of the suicide, and the only one to whom she herself had confided her intention. People crowded up to him ; they almost stormed his house; but he persisted in his silence. With all the bluffness of which he was so particularly capable, he sent the importunate questioners about their business. Olga's letter he had on the very same day committed to the flames, for he feared that a court of law might require it of him. As for the rest, the cause of death was so evident that even a post-mortem examination could be dispensed with. As might have been expected, the dead girl had not succeeded in absolutely removing every trace of her deed. In the glass standing on her night-table were found, adhering to its sides, drops of a fluid whose flavour proved, even to a non-expert, that here a solution of morphia was in question. The chain of evidence became complete when in the garden, embedded under some hawthorn bushes, were found fragments of glass bottles, to the necks of which a portion of the poisonous solution still adhered in white crystal-lised streaks. They had evidently been thrown out of the window, and still bore labels giving the date of the prescription and directions for taking.

As matters stood, it would have been simple madness on the doctor's part if he had dared to attempt to hush up the suicidal intention ; for even carelessness in taking the sleeping draught was quite out of the question.

Nevertheless, he was tormented by the idea that he had been unable to carry out the dying girl's last request, and he faithfully promised himself that he would all the more truly at least keep the secret which she had wrapped round her motives for the unhappy deed.

If only he himself could see his way clear at last ! The days passed by, however, and still he could not succeed in taking possession of the legacy which Olga had left to him.

Mrs. Hellinger, senior, mistrusted him ; she told him openly to his face that he had always had some secret understanding with the dead girl, and behind his back she added that if he had not prescribed such unreasonably strong solutions of morphia, Olga would have been alive and happy for a long time to come. She almost went so far as to ascribe the blame of her niece's death to their old family friend.

At any rate she did not permit him henceforth to remain for one second alone in the dead girl's room. She kept the door carefully locked, and declared she would not suffer the dead girl's belongings, which to her were sacred relics, to be defiled by the touch of strange hands, or by strange glances.

Thus from hour to hour there was increasing danger that the book, in which Olga had written down her confessions, might fall into the old woman's hands.

She need only take it into her head one day to to rummage among the little collection of volumes which filled the book-shelf, and the mischief was done.

Added to this anxiety, which drove the old doctor daily to the Hellingers' house, came his growing uneasiness about Robert who, since that disastrous hour, had fallen a prey to blank, despairing lethargy. He seemed absolutely deprived of the power of speech, would endure no one near him, and even taciturnly shunned and avoided him, his old friend ; by day he roamed about in the fields, by night he sat by his child's cot, and stared down upon it with burning, reddened eyes.

So said the servants, who three times had found him in the morning in this position.

V.

THE lights round Olga's coffin had burnt down.

The guests, who for so long had surrounded the bier in solemn silence, began to move to and fro, and to look round for refreshments.

Mrs. Hellinger, who was receiving condolences, and at the same time, with a great profusion of tears and pocket handkerchiefs, extolling the virtues of the deceased, suddenly, in the midst of her grief, proved herself an attentive and liberal hostess. The guests gave a sigh of relief when the doors of the dining-room were thrown open, and from the resplendent table a sweet odour of roast meats, *compôtes* and herring salad greeted them.

Mr. Hellinger, senior, praised the Lord, and with a few privileged friends, drank the specially fine claret which he set before them in honour of the occasion. They were not yet agreed whether an innocent game of cards would be disparaging to the general mourning, and decided to send delegates to the hostess to obtain her permission.

There was plenty of life and bustle in the Hellingers' house—one might have imagined one were at a wedding.

The physician, who dropped in late upon this merry company, looked about anxiously for Robert. He was nowhere to be seen.

Thereupon he took one of the guests aside and inquired after him. Yes, he had been there, had looked about him with startled eyes, and had silently moved aside when any one wanted to shake hands with him. But after a very few minutes his disappearance had been noticed.

The physician went into the entrance-hall, and hunted among the guests' wraps for Robert's cloak. It was lying there yet.

With the freedom of an old friend of the family, he then commenced his search through the back rooms of the house, which were quiet and deserted ; for the servants were busy waiting at table.

In a narrow, dark chamber, where disused furniture was piled up, he found him sitting on an overturned wooden case, brooding with his head in his hands.

"Robert, my boy, what are you doing here?" he cried out to him.

He raised his head slowly and said, "I suppose there are merry goings-on in the other part of the house?"

The physician laid his hands on his shoulders:

"I am anxious about you, my boy.　Since three days you grudge a word to any of us ; you are on the road to madness, if you go on like this."

"What do you want?" answered Robert, with a sigh that broke from him like a cry of anguish. "I am calm, quite calm."　Then he once more rested his bushy head upon his two hands, and fell again to brooding.

The old man sat down at his side and began to remonstrate with him.　He forgot no single thing that one is won't to say in such cases, and added many a comforting, strengthening word of his own making.　Robert sat there motionless, he hardly gave any sign of interest.　But when the old man came to no stop, he interrupted him, and said :

"Leave that, uncle, that is sweet stuff for little

children. To the one question on which for me depends life and death, you, too, can give me no answer."

" What question ? "

" Uncle, see, I am calm now—wonderfully calm— no fever, no frenzy is upon me as I speak, and so you will believe me when I tell you that I do not know—how I shall live through this night ! "

" For God's sake, what are you about to do ? "

Robert shrugged his shoulders.

"I do not know," he said, "whatever suggests itself at the moment will do for me. I am only sorry for the poor little mite that will have to go on living without a father—perhaps I shall take it with me on my journey—I do not know. I only know the one thing, that I cannot go on like this any longer ! "

The old man, trembling with fear in every limb, heaped reproaches upon him. That would be cowardly, that would be unmanly, and only worthy of a miserable weakling.

Robert listened to him calmly, then he said :

" You would be right, uncle, if it were her death which made me despair of myself and of my happiness !　But, good heavens !"—he laughed harshly and bitterly—" I have long since accustomed myself to lay no claim to happiness.　As for me, I would quietly bear my affliction,—(I have experience in that, as you know, for I have already lowered one loved being into the grave),—and go on raking and scraping money together, as I have been doing for so long, and doing in the midst of the deepest sorrow ; for the interests, you know, they take little notice of the state of one's feelings, and even if one's hand grows numb with pain and despair—they have to be paid !　But that is not what makes my brain so disorganised — for I am disorganised, you may believe me ; before my eyes sparks are constantly dancing, my body is convulsed, and my blood rushes like fire through my veins.　And yet I am quite calm with it all, and see everything all around as clearly as if I could look right through it.　Only the one thing I cannot comprehend—it haunts me like a terrible phantom by day and by night, and when I seek to grasp it, it escapes me—this one thing : *Wherefore* did she die ?"

The old man started. He thought of the letter and the promise that the dead girl had therein required of him.

Robert continued : " There is a voice which constantly screams into my ears, ' It is *your* fault ! ' *How* so I do not know ; for however much I probe the depths of my soul, I find no wrong there that I did her ; and yet the voice will not be silenced. I tell myself,—' This is a fixed idea.' I tell myself, ' You are tormenting yourself ; you are a fool and wicked—wicked towards yourself and your child ;' but it is no good, uncle !—it will not be silenced. And, after all, there may be something in it, uncle ? Would Olga not be alive yet, if it were not for me ? If, on the preceding evening, things had not happened——"

He stopped, shuddering, and covered his face with his hands. Tearless sobs shook his mighty frame. Then he said : " Uncle, I cannot—I dare not think of it ; it drives me out of my senses. I feel—as if I must break and dash to pieces everything with these fists."

" And yet you must pull yourself together, my

boy," said the old man, "and tell me everything successively ; for that is the only way to throw light upon the mystery."

There ensued a silence in the dark room. The old man trembled in every limb. He saw the outlines of the massive figure that stood out darkly against the light window of the chamber; he saw the heaving of the chest which rose and sank and panted and groaned like the crater of a volcano; he felt on his skin the hot waves of breath from Robert's mouth.

" Pull yourself together, my boy," he repeated softly.

Robert waged a conflict within himself. Then he stretched himself as if with newly awakening energy and said:

"All right, uncle ; you shall know all. . . .

" Since the day on which she so proudly and coldly refused my offer I had not met her again. It is true she came as before to the manor to look after the child and the household. I know now that it was for Martha's and not for my sake ; but there was a silent understanding between us, so that we avoided meeting each other. She chose the hours when she knew I was busy out in the sheds and stables, and I did not return to the house until I had seen her disappear through the gate.

"On Tuesday, as it happened, I was obliged to go out to the manor farm; but half a mile outside the town, on that bad road, my axle broke. As I had taken no driver with me, and far and wide there was no one in sight, I myself mounted the harnessed horse and rode back to fetch help. At the manor the overseer told me that the young lady had gone home some time before. It was, in fact, already beginning to grow very dark. 'Well, then there's no danger,' I think to myself, and walk into the house.

"When I open the door of the sitting-room, I see in the dusk a dark shadow that flits hurriedly out of the room.

"'Who may that be?' I think, and follow in pursuit.

"In the child's room I find—*her*—just as she is trying hard to unbolt the door leading to the corridor, which, as you know, is always kept locked on account of the draught.

7

"Then, uncle, it comes over me as if I must rush towards her; but just in time I recollect who she is—and who I am.

"I see how her hands are trembling. 'Do not be angry with me, Olga,' I said, stammering; 'I did not wish to do you any harm. I am only here by chance. I will henceforth arrange so that you may never meet me.'

"Then she lets her hands drop, and gives me a look that makes me feel hot and cold all over. 'Martha never looked at me like that,' I think to myself. I want to speak, but the words will not come, for I am so confused and embarrassed. She stands pressing her tall figure close up to the door, as if to take refuge there from me. I hear her heavy, feverish breathing. 'Olga,' I say, 'it was presumption on my part that I ever dared to think of gaining your hand; I know very well that I am not worthy of you. I beg of you, forget all about it; I will never remind you of it.'

"And at this moment, uncle—how shall I describe it to you?—leave me for a second— the memory—yet what boots it?—I will be strong, uncle—I will pull myself together—at this moment she rushes towards me, clasps me round, covers my face with kisses, and then suddenly she sinks down with a sigh and lies there at my feet as if felled by a stroke. I gaze down upon her like one in a dream.

"'It is not true,' I cry to myself; 'it is madness. You were ready to look up to her as to a goddess, and now she throws herself away on one who is not worthy of her.'

"I hardly dared to touch her; but I had to raise her up; and when I held her in my arms she began to sob bitterly, as if she would cry her very soul out. 'Olga, why are you crying?' say I. 'All is well now.' But even I, giant of a fellow as I am, start crying like a little child.

"'Forgive, me, Robert!' I hear her voice at my ear; 'I have grieved you sorely, but I will never—never do so again.'

"'And will you always love me now?' I ask; for even now I cannot realise it yet.

"'Oh, you—you,' she says, 'I love you more than anything else in the world,' and hides her face upon my neck.

"But now, uncle, hear what followed ! When I see her dark head of curls lying so submissively upon my shoulder the question arises within me : 'Is this the same Olga who, a few days ago, turned from you so calmly and proudly when you modestly and humbly asked her consent?'

"So I said to her: 'Olga,' said I, 'how could you torture me so? Have I become a different man in this short space of time?' Then I see her grow as white as the chalk on the walls, and hear her voice in my ear: 'Do not question me; for God's sake do not question me!'

"A feeling of terror awakens within me lest I may perhaps lose her to-morrow—as I have won her to-day.

"'Olga,' say I, 'if you are so changeable in your decisions, who will give me surety——?'

"I stop short, for in her face lies something which commands silence. She tears herself away from me and flings herself into a chair.

"'As you wish to know,' she says, and the while with darkening brows stares upon the ground—'I was afraid—I doubted your love, and thought you might let me feel that I came to you without a penny——'

" And with that the lie makes her face all aflame.

"'Olga,' I cry out, 'could you think that of me? Do you remember——' What I reminded her of was one night on her father's estate when I came wooing Martha and thought to return sadly with a refusal; for Martha was ready to sacrifice herself and her happiness, so that I might marry another. Then she—Olga—had come to me in the middle of the night, and had opened my eyes for me, blind fool that I was, and spoken words to me, words full of contempt for mammon, which sounded like Love's song of triumph in my ears. *Those* words I spoke to her now; for each one was indelibly stamped on my memory.

"'At that time, then—you had such brave and generous thoughts—when you spoke on Martha's behalf,' I cried out to her, 'and now—when they apply to yourself——' I look into her face, which is trying to smile and ever smiling; but this smile grew rigid, and in the midst of it she closed her eyes and fell down fainting, like a log of wood.

"It was trouble enough to bring her back to life; for I did not care to call in any help. Quite a quarter of an hour she lay there—not much otherwise than she is lying now—then she opened her eyes, and for a long time gazed silently into my face—so sorrowfully, so wearily and hopelessly, that I quite trembled for her. And thereupon she folded her hands and spoke up to me softly and imploringly:

"'Give me time, Robert; I have overtaxed my strength. I must first grow accustomed to it——'

"I, however, was so filled with the exuberance of my new happiness that I believed I could by force compel her too to be happy. 'If we love each other, Olga,' I cried, 'and the deceased says "Yes" and "Amen" to our union, I should like to see who could object! Therefore be brave and cheerful, my child!' But she was anything but brave or cheerful. And not till now—when she is dead—have I realised how utterly miserable and broken down she was as she lay there on the cushions—she who as a rule was so proud and severe in her behaviour to herself and others. It was as if some intense sorrow had cut the innermost nerve of her life in twain. That is all clear to me now, but then I did not see it—I would not see it; and I went on remonstrating with her, comforting her as I thought. She listened to me, but said nothing; only now and then she nodded her head, and a smile of unutterable sadness and weariness played about her lips.

"I put it all down to the excitement of the moment and to the sadness of the last few years, which must rise up once more all the mightier within her, now that, for her too, a new happiness was dawning to supplant it.

"'And the first thing we do,' said I, 'Olga, shall be to visit the churchyard. When we have stood at Martha's grave, my mother's resistance and the ill-will of the whole world need no longer affect us.'

"Then she let her hands drop from her face, looked at me with great terror-stricken eyes, and asked in a perfectly toneless voice: 'You want to go to the churchyard with me?'

"'Yes, with you,' I answered; 'and now, at once, if you are willing.'

"Then a shudder ran through her frame, and in a strangely hoarse tone she said : ' Have patience till to-morrow; to-morrow I will do what you wish.'

"' Yes, my dear, good child,' I then said ; 'put all foolish fancies out of your head by to-morrow, and think to yourself that *she* is not angry with us. We shall certainly not forget her ! And must not our mutual grief for her bind us all the more closely together for the whole of our lives? Her memory will always be with us ; and do you not also believe that from her whole heart she would bless our union if she could look down upon us from heaven ? Has she not left us her child as a legacy, that we might watch over it together, and not surrender it to any stranger ? '

"Then she threw herself down in front of the little cot, in which the little creature lay blissfully dozing, and pressed her face against its little head.

"Thus she lay for a long time, and I let her lie.

"When she rose up, the rigid calm once more rested upon her face that we were wont to see there. She gave me her hand, and said: 'Go, my friend; leave me alone.' And I went, for I was ready in all things to do her bidding; I did not even embrace her.

"A quarter of an hour later I saw her cross the courtyard. I waited at the window; but she did not look back any more.

"Next morning—well, you know, uncle, how I found her then. And at that moment I was as if struck by lightning. Uncle, I may grow old and grey—that moment will destroy every pleasure, and every laugh will die away from my lips as its consequence. But at least I might live. I might drag on this miserable existence, so that my child should not be deprived of its modest share of happiness. Only that one thing I must know—I must be freed from that one horrible idea, else I cannot go on—I cannot, however hard I try. Else I shall rot away alive. . . . Some one must arise, even if it be from the other side of the grave, and must tell me wherefore she died!"

Once more there was silence in the dark room. Nothing was audible but the heavy breathing of the two men and the rustling of a rat, which had accompanied Robert's story with the monotonous, hollow music of its gnawing.

The old man struggled hard within himself. Should he treacherously disclose the secret of her life as he had already betrayed the secret of her death? But was there not, in this case, a good deed to be done? Did it not mean freeing him whom she had loved above all things, from the torments to which—either a mistaken idea or a secret consciousness of guilt—condemned him? It seemed like a miracle, like special heavenly grace, that the mouth which seemed closed for ever, should once more be permitted to open, to bring peace to the loved one.

The old man gave a deep sigh. He had taken his resolution. "And supposing she should have taken thought, Robert," he said, "to give an account to you from beyond the grave?"

Robert uttered a cry, and clutched his wrists.

"What do you mean by that, uncle?"

"If you had not burrowed in your grief like a

mole, and taken flight before every human face, you would have known long ago what is in every one's mouth, namely, that on the morning of her death I received a letter from her——"

" You—uncle—from her——? "

" Goodness, my boy, you are breaking the bones in my body. Do first listen to me patiently "—and he told him the contents of the letter.

Robert had started to his feet and was nervously running his fingers through his hair. His eyes, which were staring down upon the old man, gleamed through the darkness.

" And the book—give it to me—where is it ? "

The old man informed him how great was the danger in which Olga's secret was hovering, and what anxiety he had himself passed through on its account.

" Wait, I will fetch it," cried Robert, and hurried towards the door.

The old man held him back. " Your mother has the key—take care that her suspicion is not aroused."

" The door is half broken, I will smash it entirely."

"They will hear you downstairs."

"They are enjoying themselves much too well!" answered Robert, and laughed grimly. "Come, we will go together."

And through a back door, along the dark corridor, up the creaking stairs, the two men crept like two thieves who have come to take advantage of some festive occasion.

Opening the door proved even easier than they had hoped. The loosened hinge of the lock moved out of its joints almost without pressure.

At the door both stopped, overcome with emotion, as the dark room, faintly illumined by the starry clearness of the night, lay before their eyes. All traces of death had been removed : the empty bedstead—whose supports stood out darkly against the grey wall—alone indicated that its occupant had sought another resting-place. The odour of her dresses, the faint scent of her soap, still filled the room with their fragrance. Even the towels on which she had dried herself were still hanging, in fantastic whiteness, near the black Dutch stove.

Robert, unable to keep himself upright, dropped

down upon a chair, and in long, eager breaths, which resembled a sobbing, he drank in the fragrance of the room. It was as if he were trying to absorb into his being the very last trace of her life.

A short, dazzling gleam of light darted through the room, danced along the walls, strayed with a yellow flicker across the writing-desk, and made the white-draped dressing-table stand out from the darkness like some crouching phantom.

The old man had struck a match and was groping by its aid for the little green-shaded lamp which had lighted Olga's sleepless nights. It stood on the pedestal, in the same place where Olga had extinguished it when about to plunge into eternal night. Its glass bowl was yet nearly full of petroleum. She had been in a hurry to get to rest.

Carefully he lifted down the globe and lighted the wick. With a peaceful twilight glow the veiled flame cast its light across the silent chamber. Then he stepped up to the book-shelf, where the gilded volumes were ranged in rows and gleamed in the light. His hand for a little while groped along the wall and then pulled out to the light some blue, rolled-up object.

"We have it, Robert," he cried, triumphantly; "come away!"

The latter shook his head in silence. The old man urged him again; then he said: "We will read here, uncle—here—where she wrote it."

"What if any one should surprise us?" cried the old man, fearfully.

Robert shrugged his shoulders and pointed to the floor

The old man was satisfied; they softly drew up their chairs within light of the lamp. After this nothing was audible but the rushing of the winter wind as it swept through the leafless lime-tops, and the monotonously hoarse voice of the reader, accompanied from time to time by the chorus of the funeral party—now swelling up loudly, now dying away to a whisper.

VI.

"FORGIVE me, sister, for invoking from the grave your transfigured shade. In remembrance of the deep love you bore me, of the warmth with which my heart beat for you, suffer it, if I attempt to expiate the guilt that weighs so heavily upon me, and whose yoke I must drag along with me to the end of my days! Let me once more live through all the love and kindness you bestowed upon me, and in the memory thereof forget the horrors of loneliness that, like the breath of your tomb, chill my very bones.

"What a fool, what a wicked creature I was, to feel lonely while you yet dwelt on earth! Your love was the very air that I breathed! Your smile was the sunshine that animated me, your comforting, exhorting words were like the voice of God within us, to which we hearken reverently, without understanding. And how did I thank you, sister ?   I grew a stranger to you—in sorrow and misery I have to think of you, and the consciousness of guilt appals me when the soughing wind whispers your name in my ear. Between us there stands a wild phantom with flaming eyes—terrible and distorted, its hair encircled by snakes—stretching out its claw-like hands towards me, and separating me from you for ever. If it were no phantom, but flesh and blood, if what I committed were a sin, a crime, I would wrestle with it, I would overcome it with the last strength of my failing energy, or allow myself to be strangled in its bloody grip. But it is intangible, it melts away into empty air—a spectre that mocks me, a mist that clouds my reason, and by its poison is slowly destroying me. A wish !

 " A wish—it is nothing more !

"I wonder if you recognised it ? I wonder if it was reflected in your dying gaze ? I wonder if at your bedside, when you, good, noble soul, gave up the last breath of a life that was all love, you saw this spectre—a spectre born of envy and ingratitude, which I—miserable creature—dragged into your pure habitation ?

"If I had still my lisping childish beliefs, I would pour out the wretchedness of my soul before God, the Great and Merciful; but there is no one on earth or in heaven to take pity on me, none but your glorified image.

"Woe is me!—that, too, turns away from me, Weeping, it veils itself, when yonder demon approaches my soul! And yet, was it not human to feel as I did? Why are we not heavenly bodies, void of desire, pure and ethereal? Why are we born of dust, why do we cleave to dust, eat dust and return to dust when we have thrown off this great fraud of life? The great fraud of my life I will write down here—the fraud towards myself—towards you, and towards a third as well, who was pure and good—and who yet was the cause of it all.

*　　*　　*　　*　　*

"I was a quiet, lonely child.

"He who is always surrounded by love, and who has never known anything but love, often learns most easily to suffice to himself. And yet in my heart, too, there lay an inexhaustible store of love. I squandered it on dumb creatures,

petted the dogs, kissed the cats, and hugged the
geese. One of my passions was to play in the
stable: there I lolled about on the soft, warm
straw, under the very hoofs of my special pets,
that never did me any harm; or I climbed into
the manger, where I could sit for hours and gaze
lovingly into my friends' great brown eyes. But
my favourite place was in the dog-kennel. There
they often found me asleep at midday, and it was
no easy matter to get me out again: for Nero,
who was as a rule so quiet and good, showed
his teeth to any one, even to his master, who
came within reach of his chain on such occasions.
My tender affection extended also to the vege-
table-kingdom. The rose-trees appeared to me
like enchanted princesses, whose fate I bitterly
bewailed; the sunflowers were Catholic priests
in full canonicals, and the dahlias Polish maid-
servants with red head-dresses. Thus I succeeded
in assembling around me in the garden the whole
human world, and found the counterfeit present-
ment preferable to the original, for it submitted
in silence when I ordained its fate.

*   *   *   *   *

" The estate that my father had rented was the old feudal possession of a Polish magnate, which lay close to the Prussian frontier, on a hill whose one side sloped down gradually in a weed-grown park towards barren fields, while the other dropped down precipitately towards a rivulet, on whose opposite bank lay a dirty little Polish frontier village.

" When one stood on the brink cf the precipice one looked down upon the tumble-down shingle roofs, through the crevices of which smoke issued forth, and could see right into the midst of the wretched traffic of the miry street, where half-naked children wallowed in the gutter, women crouched idly on the doorsteps, and the men in ragged fustian coats trooped, with their spades on their shoulders, towards the alehouse.

" Verily there was little that was attractive about this small town, and the rabble of frontier Cossacks, that trotted to and fro sleepily on their cat-like nags, did not enhance its charms. But yet, to my childish eyes, it was enveloped in inexpressible glamour, the sensation of which creeps over me even to-day, when I picture to myself how, bewitched by all these wonderful visions, I sat for hours motionless on the grass, and stared down upon the throng in which the figures were no larger than the wooden dolls in my box of toys.

"I had been forbidden to go down, nor had I any desire to do so, since I had once been almost crushed to death between two wheels in the crowd of the weekly market to which my father had taken me.

"It was only delightful when from up there, raised high above the dirt and screaming, one could gaze down upon this world of ants, which seemed so tiny that, like the Creator Himself, one could command it with a look, but which grew larger and larger, and assumed weird, giant proportions the more one attempted to penetrate into it.

*　　*　　*　　*　　*

"It is remarkable that just of those persons who were most closely connected with me throughout my life, I have preserved but a vague recollection as they were at that time. Possibly because later impressions effaced these earliest ones.

" My father was a small, sturdy man, of thick-set stature, with close-cut black beard and hair, clad in high, brightly blacked boots, and a greyish-green shaggy jacket, who laughed at me when he saw me, gave me a friendly slap on the back, or pinched my arm, and then was gone again. He was always busy, poor papa; as long as he lived I never saw him give himself a moment's rest.

" Mama was then already very stout, was constantly eating sweet-stuff, and loved her afternoon nap; but she, too, was at work from morning till night, though she only reluctantly betook herself from place to place, and did not like one to hang on to her, or to bother her with questions.

" At that time another member of the family was Cousin Robert, who had been sent over by our Prussian relations to learn farming from papa; a big fellow, broad-shouldered and thick-necked, with fair tufts of beard, which I was wont to pull when he took me on his knee to instil the

A B C into me by means of bent liquorice sticks. I think we were always good friends, though he probably was no more to me than the other articled pupils ; for his picture, as he was then, has become hazy, exactly like all the others.

"Only one scene do I remember distinctly, when on a summer evening he had caught hold of Martha by her fair plaits and was racing after her, laughing and screaming, through the yard, and the house, and the garden.

"'What are you up to with Martha, you rascal ?' cried papa to him.

"'She has been vexing me,' he answered, without letting go of her, while she kept on screaming.

"'When I was your age I knew better how to revenge myself on a girl,' laughingly said papa, who always liked to have his little joke.

"'Well, how ?' he asked.

"'Oh, if you don't know that yourself!' replied papa.

"'One just gives her a kiss, Master Robert,' said an old gardener, who happened to be passing with a watering-can.

" Then I can see him yet, how he suddenly let the plaits drop from his hands, stood there suffused with blushes and did not know where to look. Papa shook with laughter and Martha ran off as fast as she could. When I tried her door, she had locked herself in. Not till supper-time did she put in an appearance again. Her hair hung in disorder over her forehead, and beneath it she looked out dreamily and scared.

" When, to-day, I compare the pale, thin, little suffering face that fills my whole soul, with yonder rosy, chubby, roguish countenance as it gleams upon me sometimes from my earliest childhood, I can hardly realise that both can have belonged to one and the same being.

" How her long fair plaits fluttered in the wind ! With what precocious housewifely care her eyes scanned the long table where we all sat together, with apprentices and inspectors, waiting to be filled —a whole collection of hungry mouths. And how lustily each one helped himself, when, with her merry smile, she offered the dishes.

" Now only do I begin to understand what a pil-grimage of suffering she had to make, now that I am myself preparing for the long, sad journey, at the end of which a lonely grave awaits me, more lonesome even than hers.

" In those days I was a child and looked up un-suspectingly to her, who became my teacher when she herself had hardly put off childish ways.

" It was at that time that our affairs began to take a downward course. Papa had to struggle against debts ; failure of crops, and floods—for three years in succession—destroyed any hope of improvement, and monetary cares gathered thicker and thicker around our home.

"In the household everything not absolutely necessary was dispensed with, our intercourse with the neighbouring estate owners was restricted, and even the old governess who had educated Martha and was now to have fulfilled her mission upon me, had to leave the estate.

" Martha, who was seven years older than I and just preparing to grow into her first long dress, stepped into her place. In this way, purely sisterly relations could not grow into existence between us. She was the protectress and I was the ward, until after we exchanged our *rôles*.

" I may have been about fourteen years old, when it struck me for the first time that Martha had strangely altered in manner and appearance. I ought, indeed, to have noticed it before, for I was accustomed to look about me with open eyes, but in the slow monotony of everyday life one easily overlooks the destruction that sorrow and time are working around us.

" Now I took heed, and saw her face grow thinner and thinner, saw that the colour faded more and more from her cheeks, and that her eyes sank deeper and deeper into dark hollows. Nor did she any longer sing, and her laugh had a peculiar tired, hoarse sound that hurt my ears so, that I was sometimes on the point of calling out to her 'Do not laugh!'

"At the same time she began to sicken; she complained of headache and spasms, and only with difficulty dragged herself about the house. Then, of course, papa and mama were bound to notice her condition too ; they packed her up in warm wraps, and, in spite of her remonstrance, drove with her to Prussia to consult a doctor. He shrugged his shoulders, prescribed steel pills and advised a change of air.

"Something else, too, he must have advised, which greatly disturbed my parents, at least papa; for mama, since a long time already, was not to be roused from her phlegmatic composure. When she dreamily gazed out into the distance, he often looked at her askance, shook his head, sighed, and slammed the door after him.

" But however much she might be suffering, she would not give up her work. As long as I can remember, I have never seen her idle even for a moment. As a child already she stood with her lesson-book at the cooking-stove, or had an eye on the wash-kitchen, while she wrote her German composition. Since she was grown up, she combined the duties of my instruction with all the cares which a large household imposes upon its manager. Mama had quite retired in virtue of her age, and allowed her to do and dispose as she pleased, if only the compôtes and other dainties won her approval.

" I, who was spoilt beyond measure by every one in the house, was ashamed of my inactivity, and endeavoured to take a part of the responsibility off Martha's shoulders; but with gentle remonstrance she dissuaded me.

"'Leave that, child,' she said, stroking my cheeks; 'you happen to be the princess of the house, you had better remain so.'

"That hurt me. I could bear anything rather than to be repulsed, when I came with my heart full to overflowing of generous resolves.

"One evening I saw her crying. I slunk out into the garden and fought a hard battle. I almost choked with my longing to help, but I could not so far conquer myself as to go up to her and put my arms consolingly about her neck. When I lay in bed, my desire to comfort her came upon me with renewed force; I got up, and in my nightdress, just as I was, I slipped out into the dark corridor.

"For a long time I stood outside her door, trembling with cold and with fear, and with my hand on the door-knob. At last I took heart and crept in softly.

"She knelt before her bed with her head pressed into the pillows. She seemed to be praying.

"I stopped at the door, for I did not venture to disturb her.

"At last she turned round, and at sight of me started up abruptly.

"' What do you want ? ' she stammered.

" I clung to her, and sobbed fit to soften the heart of a stone.

"' Child — for Heaven's sake—what is the matter with you ?' she cried.

" I was incapable of uttering a word. She, in her motherly way, took a large woollen shawl, wrapped me in it, and drew me down upon her knee, though I was then already bigger than she.

"' Now confess, my darling, what ails you ?' she asked, stroking my face.

" I gathered up all my strength, and hiding my face upon her neck, I sobbed, ' Martha—I want— to help—you.'

" A long silence ensued, and when I raised up my face I saw an unutterably bitter, sorrowful smile playing about her lips. And then she took my head between her hands, kissed my brow and said :

"' Come, I will put you to bed, child ; there is nothing the matter with me—but you—you seem to be in a perfect fever.'

" I jumped up : ' For shame, that is horrid of you, Martha,' I cried ; ' I will not be sent away like this. I am not ill, nor am I so stupid that I cannot see how you are pining away, and how each day you gulp down some new sorrow. If you have no confidence in me, I shall conclude that you do not wish to have anything to do with me, and all will be over between us.'

"She folded her hands in astonishment, and looked at me.

"'What has possessed you, child?' she said, 'I do not know you thus.'

"I turned away and bit my lips defiantly.

"'Come, come, I will put you to bed,' she urged again.

"'I don't want—I can go alone,' I said. Then she seemed to feel that a word of explanation must be vouchsafed to the child.

"'See, Olga,' she said, drawing me down to her, 'you are quite right, I have many a sorrow, and if you were older and could understand, you would certainly be the first in whom I should confide. But first you too must learn to know life——.'

"'What more do you know of life than I?' I cried, still defiantly.

"She only smiled. It cut me to the heart, this half-painful, half-ecstatic smile. A dull dawning presentiment awoke within me, such as one might experience in face of closed temple gates or distant palm-wafted islands. And Martha continued :

" ' Till then, however—and that will be long !—I must bear what oppresses me alone. Hearty thanks, sister, for your good intention; I would love you twice as much for it, if that were possible ; and now go, have your sleep out, we have much to learn to-morrow.'

" With that she pushed me out of the door.

" Like an exile I stood outside on the landing and stared at the door which had closed behind me so cruelly. Then I leant my head against the wall and wept silently and bitterly.

" Martha was henceforth doubly kind and affectionate towards me, but I would not see it. I grew reserved towards her, as she had been towards me, and deeper and deeper the bitter feeling became graven on my soul that the world did not require my love. Of course it was not this one occurrence alone which acted decisively upon my disposition. Such a young creature as I was, is too easily carried away by the tide of new impressions to be lastingly influenced by a few such moments ; and, as a matter of fact, it was not long before I had forgotten that evening. But what I did not forget was the idea that no one dwelt on earth who was willing to share his sorrows with me, and that I was thrown back upon myself and my books until such day as I should be declared ripe to take part in the life of the living.

"Deeper and deeper I dived down into the treasures of the poets, of whom none drove me from his holy of holies. I learnt to feel wretched and exalted with Tasso ; I knew what Manfred sought on icy Alpine snowfields ; with Thekla I mourned the loss of the earthly happiness I had enjoyed, of the life and love that I had out-lived and out-loved. But, above all, Iphigenia was my heroine and my ideal.

"Through her my young, lonely soul was filled with all the charm of being unintelligible ; it seemed to be the mission of my life to go forth like her upon earth as a blessed priestess, sublimely void of earthly desire ; and if to this end I might have donned yon white Grecian robes whose noble draperies would so splendidly have suited my early-developed figure, my bliss would have been complete

"Outwardly I was in those years an obstinate, supercilious creature, who was lavish with rude answers, and fond of getting up from table in the middle of a meal if anything did not suit her taste.

"In spite of all this—or perhaps just for this reason—I was petted by all, and my will, in so far as a child's will can be taken into account, was considered authoritative by the whole house. At fifteen I was as tall and as big as to-day, and already there was found here and there some gallant squire's son who would say that I was much, much better looking than all the others, especially than Martha. That made me indignant, for my vanity was not yet fully developed.

"About that time, I dreamt one night that Martha had died. When I woke, my pillows were wet through with tears. Like a criminal on that day I crept round my sister. I felt as if I had some heavy offence against her on my conscience.

"After dinner she had gone to lie down for a little on the sofa, for she was suffering again from her headache ; and when I entered the room and saw her waxen-pale face with closed eyes, hanging across the sofa-ledge, I started as if struck.

"I felt as if I really saw her already as a corpse before me.

"I dropped down in front of the sofa and covered her lips and brow with kisses. Quite radiantly she opened her eyes and stared at me, as if she saw a vision ; only as consciousness returned did her face grow serious and sad, as before.

"'Well, well, my girl, what is the matter with you ?' she said. 'This is not your usual behaviour !'

"And gently she pushed me away, so that once more I stood alone with my overflowing heart ; but as I was slinking away she came after me, and whispered—

"'I love you very much, my darling sister !'

"On the evening of the same day I noticed that she constantly kept smiling to herself. Papa was struck by it too, for as a rule it never occurred. He took her head between his two hands, and said—

"'What has come over you, Margell ? Why you are blooming like a flower to-day.'

" Then she blushed a deep red, while I secretly clasped her hand under the table, and thought to myself, 'We know very well what makes us so happy.'

" Next morning papa came to the breakfast-table with an open letter in his hand.

" ' A strange bird is about to fly into our nest,' he said, laughing ; ' now guess what his name is !' And with that he looked quite peculiarly across at Martha. She appeared to me to have grown even a shade paler, and the coffee-cup which she held in her hand shook audibly.

" ' Has the bird been in our nest before ? ' she asked slowly and softly, and did not raise her eyes.

" ' I should think so indeed !' laughed papa.

" ' Then it is—Robert Hellinger,' she said, and sighed deeply, as if after a hard effort.

" ' Upon my word, girl, you *are* one to guess,' said papa, and shook his finger at her.

" But she was silent, and walked from the room with slow, dragging steps—nor did she appear again that morning. For my part I kept pretty cool over our cousin's approaching visit. His image of former days, as it dimly hovered in my memory, was not such as to inspire a romantic imagination of fifteen years with ardent dreams for its sake.

"But Martha's behaviour had struck me. Next day, in the early morning, I heard her walking up and down with long strides in the guest-rooms.

"I followed her, for I was anxious to know what she was busying herself about in these usually closed apartments.

"She had opened all the windows, uncovered the beds, let down the curtains, and now in her wooden shoes was running amidst all this confusion from one room to the other. Her hands she held pressed to her face, and kept laughing to herself; but the laugh sounded more like crying.

"When I asked her, 'What are you doing here, Martha?' she gave a start, looked at me quite confused, and seemed as if she must first think where she was.

"'Don't you see—I am covering the beds,' she stammered after a while.

"'For whom, pray?' I asked.

"'Don't you know we are going to have a visitor?' she answered.

"' I suppose you are awfully pleased at the prospect?' I said, and slightly shrugged my shoulders.

"'Why should I not be pleased?' she replied. 'It is our cousin.'

"'And nothing more?' I asked, shaking my finger at her as I had seen papa do the day before.

"Then she suddenly grew very grave, and looked at me with her big, sad eyes so strangely and reproachfully that I felt how all the blood rushed to my face. I turned away, and as I could no longer keep up my superiority, I slunk out of the door.

"From this moment Cousin Robert caused me many a thought. It seemed clear to me that the two loved each other, and seized by the mysterious awe with which the idea of the great Unknown fills half-grown children of my age, I began to picture to myself how such a love might have taken shape. I ran through the wild-growing shrubs of the park, and said to myself, 'Here they enjoyed their secret walks.' I slipped inside the dusky arbours, and said to myself, 'Here in the moonlight was their trysting-place.' I sank down upon the mossy turf-bank, and said to myself, ' Here they held sweet converse together.' The whole garden, the house, the yard, everything that I had known since the beginning of my life suddenly appeared re-splendent in a new light. A purple sheen was spread over all. Wondrous life seemed to have awakened therein. I had so completely absorbed myself in these phantasies, that finally I believed that I myself had lived through this love. When I saw Martha again I did not dare to raise my eyes to her, as if I cherished the secret in my bosom and she were the one who must not guess it.

"But next morning when I reflected that Martha had positively experienced everything that I after all had only dreamt about, I felt quite awed by the thought, and from out of a dark corner I contem-plated her fixedly with shy, inquiring looks, as if she were a being from some strange world.

" I was well aware that every five minutes she found something to busy herself about on the verandah, from whence one could look across towards the courtyard-gate ; but to-day I took

good care not to put any pert questions to her.
Now I felt like a confidante—like an accomplice.
It was a beautiful clear September day. Over
woodland and meadow was spread a rosy veil,
silver threads floated softly through the air, the
river carried a cover of vapour, and far and wide
it was as silent as in a church. I went into the
wood, for I could never have excess of solitude to
satiate myself with dreams. In the birch-trees
faded leaves already rustled ; the bracken drooped
like a wounded human being that can barely keep
upright.

"I grew very sad. 'Now there will be a great
dying,' I said : 'ah, that one might die too !'

"And then I remembered what I had heard and
read in derision of sentimental autumn thoughts.
'For shame, how wicked !' I thought. 'They
shall not deride me, for I shall know how to
conceal myself and my feelings. It is no one's
business what I do feel. And for all I care they
may think me cold and heartless, if only I have
the consciousness that my heart beats warmly and
full of love for mankind.'

"Yes, that was a delightful, foolish day, and blissfully would I sacrifice what yet remains to me of life, if it might once more be granted to me. In the evening—I can see it all as if it were to-day—the windows stood open, the tendrils of the wild vine swayed in the breeze, and from the distance a stamping of hoofs, a clashing of lances and swords greeted my ears. I could see nothing, for the darkness devoured it all, but I knew that it was a band of Cossacks patrolling along the frontier ditch. And then I closed my eyes and dreamt that a troop of knights were coming riding along at full speed—led by a fair, handsome prince, mounted on a milk-white charger. But I was the châtelaine sitting in the turret-room of the old castle, and the fame of my beauty had penetrated to every land, so that the prince had set forth surrounded by a company of picked horsemen, to seek me out and ask my hand in marriage of the old nobleman my father.

"And then I remembered Martha; and whether, as the elder, she would not be preferred. But she loves her Robert, I comforted myself, she wants no prince. And then I pictured to myself what I would give to each member of my family when

I had mounted the throne : to Martha wonderful jewellery, to papa an iron chest full of gold, and to mama a box of pine-apple sweets.

"The clashing of lances died away in the distance—and my dream was at an end.

*   *   *   *   *

" Next day he came.

" When the carriage that brought him rolled in at the courtyard gate, Martha was busy in the kitchen. I ran to her, and beaming with pleasure I whispered into her ear, 'Martha, I believe he is here.' But she forthwith apprised me that I was not her confidante. She looked at me vaguely for a time, then asked absently, 'Whom do you mean ?'

" ' Whom else but our cousin ? '

" ' Why do you tell me that in a whisper ? ' she asked. And when, in answer, I shrugged my shoulders, she once more took up the kitchen spoon she had put down, and went on stirring.

" ' Is that the extent of your pleasure, Martha ? ' I asked, while I contemptuously pursed my lips.

" But she pushed me aside with her left hand

and said, more passionately than was her wont, ' Child, I beg of you, go !'

" And thus it came about that I received Cousin Robert in her stead.

" As I stepped out on to the verandah, he was just alighting from his carriage.

" ' He does not look much better than papa,' that was my first thought. A great strong man like a giant, with broad chest and shoulders, his face sun-burnt, with little blue eyes in it, and framed by a shaggy beard, such a beard as the ' lancequenets ' used to wear.

" ' Only the chin-strap is wanting,' I thought to myself.

" He came jumping up the steps laughing towards me.

" ' Well, good morning, Martha !' he cried.

" And then suddenly he stopped short, measured me from head to foot and stood there, half-way up the stairs, as if petrified.

" ' My name is not Martha, but Olga !' I remarked, somewhat dejectedly.

" ' Ah, that accounts for it !' he cried, shaking with laughter, stepped up to me and offered me 'a red, horny hand, quite covered with cracks and weals.

"'What an uncouth fellow!' I thought in my own mind. And when we had entered the room he looked me up and down again and said, 'You were quite a little thing yet, Olga, when I went away from here; now it seems like a wonder to me that you should be so like Martha!'

"'I like Martha,' thought I, 'when was I ever in the least like Martha?'

"'But no,' he continued, 'she was not so tall, and her hair was fairer, and she did not stand there so haughtily—and—and—did not make such serious eyes.'

"'Ah, good Heavens,' thought I, 'you first look into Martha's eyes!'

"At this moment the kitchen door opened quite, quite slowly, and through a narrow aperture she squeezed herself in. She had not taken off her white apron. Her face was as white as this apron, and her lips trembled.

"'Welcome, Robert!' she said softly behind his back, for he had turned towards me.

"At the first sound of her voice he veered round

like lightning, and then for about a minute they stood facing each other without moving, without uttering a word.

"I trembled. For two days I had lain in wait for this moment, and now it fell so wretchedly short of my expectations. Then they slowly approached each other, and kissed. This kiss too did not satisfy me. He could not have kissed *me* differently; 'only that he did not attempt that at all,' I added mentally. And then they both were silent again. My heart beat so wildly that I had to press both hands to my bosom.

"At last Martha said, 'Won't you take a seat, Robert?'

"He nodded and threw himself into the sofa-corner so that all its joints creaked. He looked at her again and again, then after a long time he remarked, 'You are very much changed, Martha!'

"I felt as if he had given me a slap in the face.

"An unutterably sad smile played about Martha's lips.

"'Yes, I suppose I am changed,' she then said.

"Renewed silence. It seemed as if a long time

were necessary for him to put a thought into words.

" 'Why did I never hear that you were ailing ?' he began again at length.

" ' That I do not know,' she replied, with bitter affability.

" ' Could you not write to me about it ? '

" ' Are we in the habit of writing to each other ? ' she asked in return.

" He gave the table an angry shove.

" ' But if one is not well—then—then—'; he did not know how to proceed.

" I pressed my fists together. I should so have liked to finish his sentence for him.

" ' Never mind,' said Martha, ' one often knows least one's self when one is not well.'

" ' I should think one ought to know that best one's self,' he replied.

" ' What if one does not think it worth while to take any notice of it ? ' This time she spoke without bitterness, modestly and quietly as she always spoke, and yet every word cut me to the quick.

" ('Oh, Martha, why did you repulse me?' a voice within me cried.)

"And thereupon she broke into a short laugh, and asked how things were at home, and whether uncle and aunt were well.

"'First I should like to know how my uncle and my aunt are,' he said, and looked into the four corners of the room.

" I was so glad to see the strained mood giving way, that I burst into a loud laugh at his comical search.

" Both looked at me in astonishment as if they only just remembered my presence.

"'And what do you say to our child?' asked Martha, taking my hand in motherly fashion, 'does she please you?'

"'Better now already,' he said, scrutinising me, 'before, she was too stiff for me.'

"'I could hardly put my arms round your neck at once?' I replied.

"'Why not?' he asked, smiling complacently, 'do you think there is no room for you there?'

"'No,' said I, to let him know at once how to take me, 'that room is not the place for me.'

"He looked at me quite taken aback, and then remarked, nodding his head—

"'By Jingo, the little woman is pretty sharp.'

"I was going to reply something, but at that moment papa entered the room.

"At table I constantly kept my eye on the two, without however being able to notice anything suspicious.

"Their eyes hardly met.

"'Afterwards when the old people are taking their nap,' I thought to myself, ' they are sure to try and make their escape.' But I was mistaken. They quietly remained in the sitting-room, and did not even seem anxious to get me out of the way. He sat in the sofa-corner smoking, she, five paces away at the window, with some needle-work.

"'Perhaps they are too shy,' I thought, 'and are waiting till an opportunity presents itself.' I marked a few signs and slipped out. Then for half an hour I crouched in my room with a beating heart and counted the minutes till I might go back again.

"'Now he will go up to her,' I said to myself, 'will take her hands and look long into her eyes. "Do you still love me?" he will ask ; and she, blushing rosy red, will sink with tear-dimmed gaze upon his breast.'

"I closed my eyes and sighed. My temples were throbbing; I felt more and more how my fancies intoxicated me, and then I went on. picturing to myself how he would drop on his knees before her and, with ardent looks, stammer forth glowing declarations of love and faithfulness.

"I knew by heart everything that he was saying to her at this moment, no less than what she was answering. I could have acted as prompter to them both. When the half-hour was over, I held counsel with myself whether I should grant them a few moments longer./ I was at present their fate and as such I smilingly showered my favours upon them.

"'Let them drain their cup of bliss to the last drop!' said I, and resolved to take a walk through the garden yet. But curiosity overpowered me so that I turned back half-way.

"Softly I crept up to the door, but hardly did I find courage to turn the handle. The thought of what I was about to see almost took my breath away.

"And what did I see now, after all?

"There he still sat in his sofa-corner as before, and had smoked his cigar down to a tiny stump; but in her embroidery there was a flower which had not been there before.

"'Why do you shrug your shoulders so contemptuously?' asked Martha, and Robert added, 'It seems I do not meet with her ladyship's gracious approval.'

"'So,' thought I, 'for all my kindness I get sneers into the bargain,' and went out slamming the door after me. That same night, I, foolish young creature that I was, lay awake till nearly morning, and pictured to myself how I, Olga Bremer, would have behaved had I been in the place of those two. First I was Robert, then Martha; I felt, I spoke, I acted for them, and through the silence of my bedroom there sounded the passionate whisperings of ardent, world-despising love.

"As things were much too straightforward to please me, I invented a number of additional obstacles—our parents' refusal, nocturnal meetings at the frontier trench, surprise by the Cossacks, imprisonment, paternal maledictions, flight, and finally death together in the waves ; for only hereby, so it seemed to me, could true love be worthily sealed and confirmed.

" When I got up in the morning my head whirled, and yellow and green lights danced before my eyes.

" Martha clasped her hands in horror at my appearance, and Robert, who was sitting again for a change in a sofa-corner, and once again sending forth clouds of smoke all around, remarked—

" ' Have you been crying or dancing all night ? '

" ' Dancing,' I replied, ' on the Brocken, with other witches.'

" ' One positively cannot get a sensible word out of the girl,' he said, shaking his head.

" ' As you cry into the wood,' replied I.

" ' Oh ! I am as still as a mouse already,' he remarked, laughing, ' else I shall get such a dish of aspersion to begin the day with, as I have never swallowed in all my life.'

" Martha looked at me reproachfully, and I ran out into the park where it was darkest and hid my burning face in the cool mass of leaves.

10

"I was near crying.

"'So this is my fate,' I moaned, 'to be misunderstood by the whole world, to stand there alone and despised though my heart is full of passionate love, to wither unheeded. in some corner, while every other being finds its companion and stills its longings in an ardent embrace.'

"Yes, I had so vividly pictured to myself Martha's love that I had finally come to think myself the heroine of it.

"Thus, of course, disenchantment could not fail to come.

"And if only the two had made some further effort to keep pace with the flights of my imagination! But the longer Robert remained in our house, the more I watched Martha's intercourse with him, the more did I become convinced that all interest was unnecessarily wasted upon them.

"She—the type of a timid, insipid, housewife, subject to any fatality of every-day life.

"He—a clumsy, dull, work-a-day fellow, incapable of any degree of emotion.

"In this strain I philosophised as long as the bitter feeling that I was unnoticed and superfluous wholly filled my soul. Then there came an event which not only disposed me to be more lenient, but also gave a new direction to my ideas about this stranger cousin.

*   *   *   *   *

"It was on the fourth day of his visit when he unexpectedly stepped up to me and said:

"' Little one, I have a request to make to you. Will you come out for a ride with me?'

"' What an honour,' replied I.

"' No, you must not begin again like that,' said he, laughing, though annoyed. 'We will try for once to be good comrades just for half an hour. Agreed?'

"His cordiality pleased me. I gave him my hand upon it.

"As we rode out of the courtyard gate Martha stood at the kitchen window and waved to us with her white apron.

"' See here, Martha,' I thought in my mind, 'this is how I would ride out into the wide world with him if I were his paramour.'

"For my ideas as to what a 'paramour' is

were as yet very vague, and I did not hesitate to ascribe this dignity to Martha.

"'He rides well,' I went on thinking; 'my prince could not do better.'

"And then I caught myself throwing myself back proudly and joyously in my saddle, swayed by an undefined sense of well-being that made all my nerves tingle.

"He said nothing, only now and again turned towards me and nodded at me smilingly, as if he thought well to secure our compact anew every five minutes. It was needless trouble, for nothing was further from my thoughts than to break it.

"When we had ridden for half an hour at a sharp trot he pulled up his chestnut and said :

"'Well, little one ?'

"'What is your pleasure, big one ?'

"'Shall we turn back ?'

"'Oh, no.'

"I was absolutely not willed to give up so quickly what filled me with such intense satisfaction.

"'Well, then, to the Illowo woods,' said he, pointing to the bluish wall which bordered the distant horizon.

" I nodded and gave my horse the whip, so that it reared up high and plunged along in wild bounds.

"' Very creditable for a young lady of fifteen,' I heard his voice behind me.

"' Sixteen, if you please ! ' cried I, half turning round towards him. ' By the bye, if you again reproach me with my youth, there's an end to our good fellowship.'

"' Heaven forbid ! ' he laughed, and then we rode on in silence.

" The wood of Illowo is intersected by a small rivulet, whose steep banks are so close together that the alder branches from either side intertwine and form a high-vaulted, green dome over the surface of the water, terminating at each bend in a dense wall of foliage, behind which it builds itself up anew. Down there, close to the water's edge, I had known, since my childhood, many a secluded nook, where I had often sat for hours, reading or dreaming to myself, while my horse peacefully grazed up in the wood.

"As we now rode slowly along between the trees, a desire seized me to show him one of my sanctuaries.

"'I want to dismount,' I called out to him; 'help me out of my saddle.'

"He jumped off his horse and did as I had bid.

"'What do you intend to do?' he then asked.

"'You will see shortly,' said I. 'First of all, let the horses go.'

"'I should think so, indeed,' he laughed. 'You seem to be one of those who catch their hares by putting salt on their tails.'

"And he set about tying the bridles to a tree.

"'Let loose,' I commanded; and as he did not obey, I gave the horses a lash of the whip, so that before he thought of catching hold of the reins tighter, they were already galloping about at liberty in the wood.

"'What now?' said he, and put his hands in his pockets. 'Do you think they will let themselves be caught?'

"'Not by you!' laughed I, for I was sure of my favourites.

"And when at a low whistle from my lips they both came racing along from the distance and snuffled about affectionately at my neck with their nostrils, my heart swelled with pride that there were creatures on earth, though only dumb animals, who bowed to my might and were subject to me through love; and triumphantly I looked up at him as if now he must know me as I really was, and what I required of the world.

"But I could see that even now I had not impressed him. 'Well done, little one!' he said, nothing more, patted me on the shoulder in fatherly manner, and then threw himself down carelessly upon the grass. The sun's rays, which broke through the foliage, glittered in his beard. Like a hero in repose he appeared to me, like those described in northern saga.

"But just as I was about to grow absorbed in my romancing, he began to yawn most fearfully, so that I was very quickly and rudely transferred to prose.

"'But we are not going to stay here, Sir Cousin.'

"'Don't be foolish, little one,' said he, closing his eyes; 'do like me, let us sleep.'

"Then a frolicsome mood possessed me, and I stepped up to him and shook him soundly by the collar.

"He snatched at my dress, but I evaded him, so

that he jumped to his feet and attempted to lay hold of me. Then I walked quietly to meet him and said, 'That's right, now come along.' And then I led him right through a dense thicket of thorns, down the steep slope, at the foot of which the deep water lay like a dark mirror. Down there broad-leaved convolvuli and creepers had formed a natural bower above a projecting block of stone, in which even at high noon one could sit almost in the dark.

"Thither I led him.

"'Upon my word, it is delightful here, little one,' he said, and comfortably stretched himself upon the stone, so that his feet hung down to the water. 'Come, sit down at my side; . . . there is room for us both.'

"I did as he wished, but seated myself so that I could look down upon him.

"He pretended to be sleeping, and now and again blinked up at me through half-closed lids.

"Then the thought suddenly came to me, 'Now, if you were Martha, what should you do?' and I was so startled by it that my blood gushed up hotly into my face.

"'Are you easily frightened, little one?' he asked.

"I shook my head.

"'Then come here!'

"'I am here at your side.'

"'Place yourself in front of me.'

"I did so. My feet almost touched the flat edge of the stone.

"Suddenly he raised himself, clasped me as quick as lightning about the waist, and at the same moment I felt myself suspended in mid-air above the water. I looked at him and laughed.

"'Let me tell you,' said he, 'that it is not by any means a laughing matter. If I let you drop——'

"'I shall be drowned—so let me drop.'

"'No, first you must make a confession to me.'

"'What confession?'

"'Why you do not like me.'

"I drew a deep breath. At the same time I felt that the soles of my feet were already being wetted by the surface of the water. He must not let me sink any lower. A delicious feeling of powerlessness came over me.

"'I do like you,' I said.

"'Then why do you give me such disagreeable answers?'

"'Because I am a disagreeable creature.'

"'That is certainly plausible,' laughed he, and with rapid swing lifted me up like a feather so that I came to stand once more upon the stone. 'There, now sit down, we will talk sensibly.' Then he took my hand and continued: 'See, I am a simple fellow, have worked hard and given little thought to sharpening my wit. You with your quick little brain always kill me at the very first thrust, so that I have grown positively afraid of talking to you. I know you mean no harm, for it is not in our blood to be ill-natured; but all the same, it is not the proper thing. I am nearly twelve years older than you, and you almost a child yet. Am I right?'

"'You are right,' said I, dejectedly, wondering privately where my defiance had departed to.

"'Then why did you do it?'

"'Because I wanted to gain your approval,' said I, and drew a deep breath.

"He looked into my eyes amazed.

"'Because I wanted to show you that I was not a silly thing, that my head was in its right place, that I——,' I stopped short and grew ashamed of myself.

"He chewed his beard and looked meditatively before him.

"'Indeed, now,' he said, 'I was in a fair way to get quite a wrong idea of your character. What a good thing that I followed Martha's advice!'

"'Martha's?' I exclaimed. 'What did she advise you?'

"'Take her aside alone some time,' she said, 'and have it out with her. Whomever she does not love she hates, and it would pain me if she did not grow to love you.'

"'Did she say that?' asked I, and tears came into my eyes. 'Oh, you good sister, you noble soul!'

"'Yes, she said that and much more besides, in order to explain and vindicate your disposition. And as I love Martha——'

"'Do you?' I interrupted him, eager to learn more.

"'Yes, very dearly,' he replied reflectively, and looked down into the water beneath him.

"My heart beat so violently that I could hardly draw my breath. So he, he took me into his confidence, he made a confederate of me. I could have embraced him there and then, so grateful did I feel towards him.

"'And does she know it?' I inquired.

"'I daresay she knows it,' he remarked; 'a thing of that sort cannot be concealed——'

"What—then—you have not—told her?' I stammered.

"He shook his head sadly.

"I was awakened from all my illusions. So the arbours of our garden had never afforded shelter to two lovers, the moon as it shone through the branches had never been the witness of clandestine kisses? And all my romancing had proved itself nothing but idle imagination? But in the midst of my disillusion a deep compassion seized me for this giant, crouching beside me as helpless as a child. Surely, I vowed to myself, he shall not in vain have put his trust in me!

"'Why did you remain silent?' I inquired further.

"He looked somewhat suspiciously at my immature youth, and then began, heaving a deep breath :—

"'You see, at that time I was a silly young fellow, and could not pluck up courage to speak ; in the years of one's youth one is already so supremely happy if one can only now and again secure a secret pressure of the hand, that one thinks marriage can have no further bliss to offer. But——you really cannot understand all these things.'

"'Who knows?' replied I, in my innocence ; ' I have read a great deal on the subject already.'

"'The short and the long of it is,' he continued, 'that I was then nearly as foolish as you are at present. And now, you see, if I speak to her now, every word binds me with iron fetters to all eternity.'

"'And don't you wish to bind yourself?' I asked in astonishment.

"' I *may* not,' he cried ; ' I dare not, for I do not know if I can make her happy.'

"'Well, of course, if you do not know that,' said I, drawing up my lips contemptuously, and in my heart I inferred further : 'Then he cannot love her either.'

"But he started up with sparkling eyes : 'Understand me aright, little one,' he cried ; 'if it only depended on me, I would ask nothing better all my life, than to carry her in my arms, lest her foot might dash against a stone. But—oh, this misery —this misery !' And he tore his hair, so that I grew quite frightened of him. Never should I have thought it possible for this quiet, reflective man to behave so passionately.

"'Confide in me, Robert,' said I, placing my hand on his shoulder ; 'I am only a foolish girl, but it will unburden your heart.'

"'I cannot,' he groaned, 'I cannot !'

"'Why not ?'

"'Because it would be humiliating—for you too. Only this much I will tell you : Martha is a delicate, tender, sensitive creature ; she would never be able to hold her own against the flood of cares and misfortune which must pour down upon her there. She would be broken like a weak blade of corn at the first onset of the storm. And what good would it be, if a few years after our wedding I had to carry her to her grave ?'

"A cold shudder runs through me, when I think

how that word of presage came to be so terribly realised ; but at that moment there was nothing to warn me. I only felt the ardent desire to give as romantic a turn as possible to this, to my mind, much too prosaic love affair. Unfortunately there was not much to be done at present. So at least I assumed a knowing air, and sought in my memory for some of the phrases with which worthy sibyls and father confessors are wont to feed the soul of unhappy lovers.

"And he, this big child, drank in the foolish words of comfort like one dying of thirst.

"'But will she have patience?' he asked, and showed signs of becoming disheartened again.

"'She will! Depend upon it,' I cried, eagerly ; 'as she has waited so long, she will wait for another year or two. You will see how gladly she will submit.'

"'And what if even later nothing should come of it?' he objected, 'if I should have disappointed her hopes, have played the fool with her heart? No, I will not speak ; they may drag my tongue out of my mouth, but I will not speak !'

"'If you did not intend to speak, why then did

you come?' asked I. Heaven knows how this two-edged idea got into my foolish young girl's head. I felt darkly that I was committing a cruelty when I put it into words, but now it was too late. I saw how his face grew pale, I felt how his breath swelled up hot and heavy and poured itself forth upon me in a sigh.

"'I am an honest man, Olga,' he muttered between his teeth; 'you must not torture me. But as you have asked, you shall have an answer. I came because I could bear life without her no longer, because by a sight of her I wanted to gather up strength and comfort for sad days to come, and because—because in my heart of hearts I still cherished the faint hope that things might be different here, that it might be possible for her to come with me.'

"'And is it not possible?'

"'No! Do not ask why; let it suffice you that I say no.'

"Then suddenly he bent down towards me, took hold of both my hands, and said, from the very depths of his soul: 'See, Olga, more has come of our good fellowship than we both could suspect an hour ago. Will you now stand by me faithfully, and help me as much as lies in your power?'

"'I will,' said I, and felt very solemn the while.

"'I know you are no longer a child,' he went on; 'you are a sensible and brave girl and do not swerve from anything you undertake. Will you keep watch over her, so that she does not lose heart, even if I now go away again in silence. Will you?'

"'I will!' I repeated.

"'And will you sometimes write to me, to tell me how she is? Whether she is well, and of good courage? Will you?'

"'I will!' I said, for the third time.

"'Then come, give me a kiss, and let us be good friends, now and always.' And he kissed me on my mouth. . . .

"Five minutes later we were on our horses and riding hurriedly towards the home farm; for it already was beginning to grow dark.

"'You stayed away a long time,' said Martha, who was standing in her white apron on the verandah, and smiled at us from afar. When I saw her, I felt as if I could never find enough tenderness to pour out upon my sister. I hastened towards her and kissed her passionately, but at the same moment I regretted it, for it appeared to me as if I were thereby wiping his kiss from my lips.

"Embarrassed, I desisted, and slunk away. At supper I constantly hung upon his eyes, for I thought he must make known our secret understanding by some sign. But he did not think of any such thing. Only when we shook hands after the meal he pressed mine in quite a peculiar way, as he had never done before. I was as pleased as if I had received some valuable present.

"On that evening I could hardly await the time when I might go to bed and put out the light; then I was often wont to stare for an hour at a time into the darkness, dreaming to myself. It was in my power to keep awake as long as I wished, and to go to sleep as soon as I thought it time. I had only to bury my head in the pillows and I was off. To-day I stretched myself in my bed with a sense of well-being such as I had never before in my life experienced. I felt as if every wish of my life had been fulfilled. My cheeks burnt, and on my lips there still distinctly remained the slight tingling sensation of that kiss—the first kiss with which a man,—papa of course did not count—had kissed me.

" And if, strictly speaking, it had been meant for some one else, what did that matter to me ? I was still so young I could not yet lay claim to anything of the kind for my own self.

" Thereupon I once more fell into my favourite reverie as to what I should do if I were in Martha's place. Thus I had no need to destroy the fancies which to-day had been proved only idle chimera, but could go on spinning them out to my heart's content, and I did spin them out, waking and sleeping, till early morning.

" Two days later he drove off. A few hours before he took his leave, he had a long con-ference with Martha in the garden. Without any feeling of jealousy I saw them disappear together, and it afforded me unspeakable pleasure to keep watch at the gate so that no one should surprise them.

" When they appeared again they were both silent, and looked sad and serious.

"No, he had not declared himself; that I saw at the first glance, but he had spoken of the future, and probably interspersed many a little word of modest hope.

"Before he stepped into the carriage, it so happened that he was for a few moments alone with me. Then he took my hand and whispered:

"'You will not betray one single word, will you? I can depend upon it?'

"I nodded eagerly.

"'And you will write to me soon?'

"'Certainly.'

"'Where shall I send the answer?'

"I started. I had not in the remotest degree thought of that. But as the moment pressed, I mentioned at haphazard the name of an old inspector who had always been specially attached to me.

* * * * *

"Time passed. One day followed another in the old way, and yet now how differently, how peculiarly the world had shaped itself for me.

"I no longer had any need to study love from

books, and search for it afar off; it had stepped
bodily into my existence, its sweet mysteries
played around me, and I—oh, joy!—I was join-
ing in the game. I was entangled head over ears
in the intrigue that was to lay the basis of my
sister's happiness.

" It was like a miracle to see how after each of
Robert's visits she revived and gained fresh strength
and colour and health. Like an invigorating bath
those few days of their intercourse had acted upon
her, and more even than they, probably, that
miraculous fountain of hope from which she had
drunk a long and furtive draught.

"Certainly the sunny cheerfulness of other days
did not return to her again, that seemed irretriev-
ably lost in those seven years of weary waiting;
no song, no laughter ever issued from her lips, but
over her features there lay spread a soft warm glow,
as if a light from within her soul irradiated them.
Nor did she any longer drag herself about the house
with lagging, weary steps, and whoever approached
her was sure of a friendly smile.

" And as her happiness must needs find vent in
love, she also attached herself more closely to me,

and tried to gain an insight into my hidden and lonely thoughts. I loved her the more dearly for it, I all the more often invoked God's blessing upon her, but I did not give her my confidence.

"Before she, of her own accord, opened out her whole heart to me, I could not and would not confess how far I had already gazed into its depths.

"Sometimes I caught myself looking across at her with a motherly feeling—if I may call it so—for since I carried on an active correspondence with Robert, I imagined that it was I who held her happiness in my hands.

"My vanity made of me a good genius, clad in white raiment, whose hand bore a palm-branch, and whose smile dispensed blessings. And meanwhile I counted the days till a letter from Robert came, and ran about with glowing cheeks when at length I carried it near my heart.

"These letters had become such a necessity to me that I could hardly imagine how I should ever be able to exist without them. Under pretext of telling him all about Martha, I most cunningly understood how to prattle away the cares that filled his heart—childishly and foolishly (as men like to hear it from us, so that they may feel themselves our superiors), and again at other times seriously and knowingly beyond my years—just as I felt in the mood. He willingly submitted to my chatter in all its different keys, as one submits to the piping of a singing-bird, and more I did not ask. For I was already so grateful that he allowed me—a silly young girl who had still to leave the room when grown-up people had serious questions to discuss—to participate in his great, grave love. All my dignity and self-consciousness were based upon this *rôle* of guardian. And thus I grew up with and by this love, of which never a crumb might fall for me beneath the table.

*   *   *   *   *

"When the following autumn approached, I noticed that Martha manifested a peculiar restlessness. She ran about her room with excited steps, remained for half the nights at the open window, gesticulated and spoke loudly when she thought herself alone, and was violently startled whenever she found herself caught in the act.

"I faithfully informed Robert of what I saw,

and added the question whether he had perhaps held out any hope of his coming at this particular time; for Martha's whole condition seemed to me to be produced through painfully overwrought expectation.

"I had every reason to be satisfied with the shrewdness of my seventeeen years, for my observations proved correct.

"Deeply contrite, he wrote to me that he had indeed at parting expressed a hope of being able to return with a cheerful face in the following autumn, but that he had deceived himself, that he was more encumbered by cares and debts than ever before, that he was working like a common labourer, and did not see a ray of hope anywhere.

"'Then at least release her from the torture of waiting,' I wrote back to him, 'and cautiously inform our parents how you are placed.'

"He did so ; two days later already, papa, in a bad humour, brought the letter along, which I—on account of my childish want of judgment—was not allowed to read.

"On Martha it operated in a way which terrified and deeply moved me. The excitement of the last weeks there and then disappeared. In its place there showed itself again that despairing listlessness which once before, in the days preceding Robert's coming, had worn her to a shadow ; once more she fell away ; once more deep blue rings appeared round her eyes ; once more an odour of valerian proceeded from her mouth while she often writhed in pain. Added to this was the constant desire to weep, which at the smallest provocation, found vent in a torrent of tears.

" This time papa did not send for a doctor. He could make the diagnosis himself. Even mama suffered with the poor girl, as far as her phlegmatic nature permitted, and it did not permit her to stir from her chimney-corner to tender help to her sickening daughter. As for me, I now for the first time found an opportunity of proving to my family that I was no longer a child, and that even in serious matters, my will claimed consideration. I took the burden of housekeeping upon my shoulders, and though they all smiled and remonstrated, and though Martha declared time after time that she would never suffer me, the younger one, to usurp her place, I had still in a fortnight, so far gained my point that the entire household danced to my pipe.

"That was the only time when Martha and I ever came to hard words ; but gradually she necessarily perceived that what I did was only done for her sake, and finally she was the first to feel grateful to me. In several other things too, she learnt to submit to me ; but she sought to deceive herself as to my influence by remarking that one must give way to children.

"Through my intercourse with Robert, I now learnt for the first that one may tell lies for love's sake. I concealed from him the sad effects of his letter, yes, I even unblushingly wrote to him that everything was as well as could be. I acted thus, because I reflected that the truth would plunge him into a thousand new cares and anxieties, which must absolutely crush him, as he was powerless to help. But it was very hard for me to keep up my light chatty tone, and often some joke seemed to freeze in my pen.

"And things grew more and more troubled. Papa was despondent because failure of crops had destroyed his best prospects, mama grumbled because no one came to amuse her, and Martha faded away more and more.

"Christmas drew near—such a gloomy one as our happy home had never before witnessed.

"Round the burning Christmas tree which I had this time trimmed and lighted in Martha's stead, we stood and did not know what to say to each other for very heaviness of heart. And because no one else did so, I had to assume a forced smile and attempt to scare the wrinkles from their brows. But I got very little response indeed, and finally we shook hands and said 'good-night,' so that each might retire to his room, for we felt that anyhow we could not get on together.

"When I came to Martha, who sat silently in a corner, gazing vacantly at the dying candles, a painful feeling darted through my breast, as if I were committing some wrong towards her, which I ought to redress. But I did not know what this wrong could be.

"She kissed me on my forehead and said: 'May God ever let you keep your brave heart, my child; I thank you for every joke to which you forced yourself to-day.' I, however, knew not what to reply, for that consciousness of guilt, which I could not grasp, was gnawing at my soul. When I was alone in my room, I thought to myself, ' There, now you will celebrate Christmas.' I took Robert's letters out of the drawer where I kept them carefully hidden, and determined to read at them far into the night.

"The storm rattled my shutters, snow-flakes drifted with a soft rustle against the window-panes, and above, there peacefully gleamed the green-shaded hanging lamp.

"Then, as I comfortably spread out the little heap of letters in front of me, I heard next door, in Martha's room, a dull thud and thereupon an indistinct noise that sounded to me like praying and sobbing.

"'That is how *she* celebrates Christmas,' I said, involuntarily folding my hands, and again I felt that pang at my heart, as if I were acting deceitfully and heartlessly towards my sister.

"And I brooded over it again till it became clear to me that the letters were to blame.

"'Do I not write and keep silence all for her good?' I asked myself; but my conscience would not be bribed ; it answered : ' No.'   Like flames of fire my blood shot up into my face, for I recognised with what pleasure my own heart hung upon those letters.   ' What would she not give for one of these papers ? '   I went on thinking, ' She who perhaps no longer believes in his love, who is wrestling with the fear that he only did not come because he meant to tear asunder the ties that bind him to her heart.' ' And you hear her sobbing ? ' the voice within me continued, ' you leave her in her anguish, and meanwhile comfort yourself with the knowledge that you share a secret with him, with him who belongs to her alone ? '

" I clasped my hands before my face ; shame so powerfully possessed me, that I was afraid of the light which shone down upon me.

" ' Give her the letters ! ' the voice cried suddenly, and cried so loudly and distinctly that I thought the storm must have shouted the words in my ears.

" Then I fought a hard battle ; but each time my good intention wavered, hard pressed by the fear of breaking my word to him, and by the wish to remain still longer in secret correspondence with him, her sobbing and praying reached me more distinctly and confused my senses so, that I felt like fleeing to the ends of the earth in order to hear no more.

"And at length I had made up my mind. I carefully packed the letters together in a neat little heap, tied them round with a silk ribbon, and set about carrying them across to her.

"'That shall be your Christmas present,' said I, for I remembered that this year I had not been able to embroider or crochet anything for her, as had usually been the custom between us. And as he who gives likes to clothe his doings in theatrical garb in order to hide his overflowing heart, I determined first to act a little comedy with her.

"I crept, half-dressed as I was, down into the sitting-room, where our presents were spread under the Christmas tree, groped in the dark for her plate, gathered up what lay beside it, and on the top of all placed the little packet of letters. Thus laden, I came to her door and knocked.

"I heard a sound like some one dragging himself up from the floor, and after a long while— she was probably drying her eyes first—her voice was heard at the door, asking who was there and what was wanted of her.

"'It is I, Martha,' I said, 'I come to bring you—your plate—you left it downstairs.'

"'Take it with you into your room, I will fetch it to-morrow,' she replied, trying hard to suppress the sobs in her voice.

"'But something else has been added' said I, and my words too were almost choked with tears.

"'Then give it me to-morrow,' she replied, 'I am already undressed.'

"'But it is from me,' said I.

"And because, despite her misery, in the kindness of her heart she did not want to hurt my feelings, she opened the door. I rushed up to her and wept upon her neck, while I kept tight hold of the plate with my left hand.

"'Whatever is the matter with you, child?' she asked, and patted me. 'A little while ago you seemed the only cheerful one, and now——'

"I pulled myself together, led her under the light, and pointed to the plate. At the first glance she recognised the handwriting, grew as white as a sheet, and stared at me like one possessed, out of eyes that were red with weeping.

"'Take them, take them!' said I.

"She stretched out her hand, but it shrank back as at the touch of red-hot iron.

"'See, Martha!' said I, with the desire to revenge myself for her silence, and at the same time to brag a little, 'you had no confidence in me; you considered me too childish, but I saw through everything, and while you were fretting, I was up and doing.' Still she continued to stare at me, without power of comprehension. 'You imagine that he no longer cares about you,' I went on, 'while all the time I have had to give him regular account of your doings and of the state of your health. Every week——'

"She staggered back, seized her head with both her hands, and then suddenly a shudder seemed to pass through her frame. She stepped close up to me, grasped my two hands, and with a peculiarly hoarse voice she said, 'Look me in the face, Olga! Which of you two wrote the first letter?'

"'I,' said I, astonished, for I did not yet know what she was driving at.

"'And, you—you betrayed to him the state of my feelings—you—*offered* me, Olga?'.

"'What puts such an idea into your head?' said I. 'He himself confessed everything to me when he was here. Oh, he knew me better than you,' I added, for I could not let this small trump slip by. 'He was not ashamed to confide in me.'

"'Thank God!' she murmured with a deep sigh, and folded her hands.

"'But now come, Martha,' said I, leading her to the table, 'now we will celebrate Christmas.'

"And then we read the letters together, one after the other, and from one and all his heart, faithful and true as gold, shone forth through the simple, awkward words, and spread a warm glow, so that our heavily oppressed souls grew lighter and more cheerful, that we laughed and cried with cheek pressed to cheek, and almost squeezed our hands off in the mutual attempt to make each other feel the pressure which his warm red fist was wont to give.

"And then suddenly—it was at one place where he specially impressed upon me to be sure and take great care of her and watch over her and protect her for his sake—her happiness overwhelmed her, and—I blush to write it down—

12

she fell on her knees before me and pressed her lips to my hand.

"But, though I was much startled, I no longer felt anything of that pricking and gnawing which a little while before, under the Christmas tree, had so sorely beset my bosom. I knew that my guilt was blotted out, and with a free light heart I vowed to myself now indeed to watch like a guardian angel over my sister, who was so much more feeble and in want of direction than I, the foolish and immature child. And she felt this herself, for unresistingly she, who had hitherto treated me as a child, submitted to my guidance.

"At last I had attained the desire of my heart. I had a human being whom I could pet and spoil as much as I pleased; and, now that every barrier between us had fallen, I lavished upon my sister all the tenderness which had for so long been stored up unused within me.

"Father and mother were not a little surprised at the newly-awakened cordiality of our relations to each other, that just latterly had left much to be desired, and Martha herself could hardly grow accustomed to the change. She contemplated me every day in new astonishment, and often said, 'How could I suspect that there was so much love within you?'

"If she could only have known what a sacrifice it cost me to divulge my secret, she would have put a still higher value upon my love.

"Yes, I had rightly guessed how it would be: from the moment when Martha had held the letters in her hand, the happiness of my secret understanding with Robert was at an end for me. Like a stranger he now appeared to me, and when I sat down to write to him I felt like a mere machine that has to copy other people's thoughts. Often I even passed on a letter unread to Martha as soon as I received it from the inspector's hands. Sometimes it worried me that I had abused his confidence to such an extent, for he suspected nothing of her knowledge; but when I looked at her, saw her newly-awakening smile and the quiet, dreamy happiness that shone forth from her eyes, I consoled my conscience with the thought that I could not possibly have committed any wrong. So far I had only become his betrayer; soon I was to betray Martha too.

"Winter and spring passed by swiftly, and the time came for storing the sheaves in the barns.

"As soon as the harvest was over he intended to come; but before then, he wrote, there was many a hardship to be surmounted.

*   *   *   *   *

"One day papa appeared in the kitchen, where we were, with an apparently indifferent air, snuffled about for a while among the pots and pans, and meanwhile kept on slashing at the long leggings of his water-boots with his riding-whip.

"'Why you have become a Paul Pry to-day, papa?' said I.

"He gave a short laugh and remarked, 'Yes, I have become a Paul Pry.' And when he had for some time longer been running backwards and forwards without speaking, he suddenly stopped in front of Martha and said—

"'If you should just have time, my child, you might come into the room for a moment. Mama and I have something to say to you.'

"'Ah, I see,' said I, 'that is the reason for this long preliminary. May I come too?'

"'No,' he replied. 'You remain in the kitchen.'

"Martha gave me a long look, took off her apron, and went with him to the sitting-room.

"For a while all remained quiet in there. Round about me the steam was hissing, the pots were broiling, and one of the maids was making a great clatter cleaning knives; but all this noise was suddenly penetrated by a short, piercing cry which could only proceed from Martha's lips.

"Trembling I listened, and at the same moment papa came rushing into the kitchen, calling for 'Water!' I hurried past him, and found my sister lying fainting on the ground with her head in mama's lap.

"'What have you been doing to Martha?' I cried, throwing myself on my knees beside her.

"No one answered me. Mama, as helpless as a child, was wringing her hands, and papa was chewing his moustache, to suppress his tears, as it seemed. Then, as I bent down over the poor creature, I saw a blue-speckled sheet of paper lying beside her on the floor, which I immediately, and unobserved by any one, appropriated.

"Thereupon I quickly did what was most pressing: I recalled my sister to consciousness, and led her, while she gazed about with vacant eyes, up to her room.

"There I laid her upon her bed. She stared up at the ceiling, and from time to time wanted to drink. Her spirit did not yet seem to have awakened again at all.

"I meanwhile secretly drew the letter from my pocket, and read what I here record verbally; for I have carefully preserved this monument of motherly and sisterly affection :—

"'My beloved Brother! Dearest Sister-in-law!—A circumstance of a very painful nature compels me to write to you to-day. You are, I am sure, fully convinced how much I love you, and how much my heart longs to be in the closest possible relation to you and your children. All through my life I have only shown you kindness and affection, and received the same from you. Relying on this affection I to-day address a request to you, which is prompted by the anxiety of a mother's heart. To-day my son Robert came to us and declared that he intended asking you for your daughter Martha's hand ; begging us at the same time to give our consent, with which, as a good son and also as a prudent man he cannot dispense, as unfortunately he still depends, to a great extent, on our assistance.

" ' If I might have followed the bent of my heart, I would have fallen upon his neck with tears of joy; but, unhappily, I had to keep a clear head for my son and my husband—who are both children—and was forced to tell him that on no account could anything come of this.

" ' My dear brother, I do not wish to reproach you in any way for not having been able to keep your affairs straight in the course of years—far be it from me to mix myself up in matters that do not concern me ; but as these matters now stand, your estate is encumbered with debts, and, with the exception of—as I would fain believe—an ample ' trousseau,' your daughters would not have a farthing of dowry to expect. On the other hand, my son Robert's estate is also heavily embarrassed through the payments which he had to make to us and his sisters and brothers—as well as by the mortgages which we still hold upon it, and by the interests of which we and my other children have to live—so that marriage with a poor girl would simply mean ruin to him.

"'I do not take into account that your daughter Martha must—according to your letters—be a weakly and delicate creature, and therefore appears to me utterly unfit to take cheerfully upon herself the cares of this large household and to render my son Robert happy ; the idea that she would come into his house with empty hands is in itself decisive for me, and suffices to convince me that she herself must become unhappy and make him so.

"'If your daughter Martha truly loves my son Robert, it will not prove hard for her to renounce all thoughts of a marriage with him in the interests of his welfare, provided, of course, he should still have the courage to propose to her in spite of his parents' opposition—although I do not expect such filial disobedience from him, and absolutely cannot imagine such a thing. I am convinced, my dear relations, that your brotherly and sisterly affection will prompt you to join with me in refusing your consent, now and for ever, to such a pernicious and unnatural union,

        "'Yours, with sincere love,

              "'JOHANNA HELLINGER.

"'P.S.—How have your crops turned out? Winter rye with us is good, but the potatoes show much disease.'

*   *   *   *   *

" Rage at this mean and hypocritical piece of writing so possessed me, that loudly laughing, I crumpled the sheet of paper beneath my feet.

" My laughter probably hurt Martha, for it was her moaning which at length brought me back to my senses. There she lay now, helplessly smitten down, as if shattered by the blow which should have steeled her strength for enhanced resistance. And as I gazed down upon her, tortured by the consciousness of being condemned to look on idly, there once again broke forth from my soul that sigh of former times: 'Oh, that you were—she!' But what new meaning it concealed! What then had been folly and childishness, had now developed into seriousness of purpose, ready self-sacrifice, and consciousness of strength.

"I determined to act as long as ever there was time yet. First of all, I would go to my parents, tell them what I had done, and that for a long time already I had been initiated into everything—and finally demand of them to assign to me at length that position in the family council which, in spite of my youth, was due to me.

"But I rejected this idea again. As soon as I participated in the deliberations of my family, it became my duty not to act contrary to whatever they thought good, and only if I apparently took no heed of anything, could I be working for the salvation of my poor sister according to my own plans and my own judgment.

"I very soon saw how matters lay. Each one had read in the letter what most appealed to his nature.

"Papa, quite possessed by a poor man's pride, would, after this, have thought it a disgrace to let his child enter a family where she would be looked at disparagingly. Mama, for her part, had been touched by the interspersed professions of affection, and thought that her sister-in-law's confidence ought not to be abused.

" And my sister ?

" That same night, as I kept watch at her bed-side, I felt her place her hot hand upon mine and draw me gently towards her with her feeble arm.

" ' I have something to say to you, Olga,' she whispered, still looking up at the ceiling with her sad eyes.

" ' Had we not better leave it till to-morrow ? ' I suggested.

" ' No,' she said, ' else meanwhile that will happen which must not happen. Henceforth all is over between him and me.'

" ' You little know him,' said I.

" ' But I know myself,' said she. ' I break it off.'

" ' Martha ! ' I cried, horrified.

" ' I know very well,' she said, ' that I shall die of it, but what does that matter ? I am of very little account. It is better so, than that I should make him unhappy.'

" ' You are talking in a fever, Martha,' I cried, ' for I do not think you silly enough to let yourself be baited by the trash of that old hag.'

" ' I feel only too well that she speaks the truth,' said she. A cold shudder passed through me when

I heard her pronounce these despairing and hopeless words as calmly and composedly as if they were a formula of the multiplication table. 'Do not gainsay me,' she continued ; 'not only since to-day do I know this—I have always felt something of the kind, and ought by rights not to have been startled to-day ; but it certainly does upset one, when one so unexpectedly sees in writing before one's eyes the death sentence which hitherto one has scarcely dared to suggest to one's own conscience.'

"As eloquently as I possibly could, I remonstrated with her. I consigned our aunt to the blackest depths of hell, and proved to a nicety that she (Martha) alone was born to become the good angel in Robert's house. But it was no good, her faith in herself would not be revived ; the blow had fallen upon her too heavily. And finally she expected it of me to write no further letter to him, and to break off our intercourse once and for all. I was alarmed to the depths of my soul, no less for my own than for her sake. I refused, too, with all the energy of which I was capable ; but she persisted in her determination, and as she even threatened to betray our correspondence to our parents, I was at length forced to comply, whether I would or no.

*   *   *   *   *

"Troubled days were in store. Martha slunk about the house like a ghost. Papa rode like wild through the woods, stayed away at meal-times, and had not a good word for any of us. Mama, our good, fat mama, sat knitting in her corner, and from time to time wiped the tears out of her eyes, while she looked round anxiously, lest any one should notice it. Yes, it was a sad time !

" Two urgent letters from Robert had arrived. He wrote that he was in great trouble, and I was to send him tidings forthwith. I told Martha nothing of them, but I kept my promise.

"A week had passed by, when I noticed that our parents were discussing what answer they would send to aunt. In order to exclude any suspicion of sneaking into a marriage, papa had the intention of binding himself by a final promise, and mama said 'yes,' as she said yes to everything that did not concern jellies and sweets.

" The same day Martha declared that she felt

unfit to leave her bed—that she had no pain, but that her limbs would not carry her.

"Thus I saw misfortune gathering more and more darkly. I dared not hesitate any longer.

"'Come! Redeem your promise before it is too late.' These words I wrote to him. And to be quite sure, I myself ran down into the town, and handed the letter to the postillion who was just preparing to start for Prussia.

"At the moment when the envelope left my hands, I felt a pang at my heart as if I had thereby surrendered by soul to strange powers.

"Three times I was on the point of returning to ask my letter back, but when I did so in good earnest the postillion was already far away.

"When I climbed up the slope leading to the manor house I hid myself in the bushes and wept bitterly.

"From that hour an agitation possessed me, such as I had never before in my life experienced. I felt as if fever were burning in my limbs—at nights I ran about my room restlessly, all day long I was on the look-out, and every approaching carriage drove all the blood to my heart.

"I gave wrong answers to every question, and the very maids in the kitchen began to shake their heads doubtfully. A bride who is expecting her bridegroom could not behave more crazily.

"This state of things lasted for four days, and it was lucky for me that each member of the family was so engrossed with himself, else suspicion and cross-examination could not have been spared me.

"This time I did not receive him. When I recognised his figure in the strange, four-horse carriage which, all besplashed with mud, tore through the courtyard gate, I ran up to the attic and hid in the most remote corner.

"My face was aglow, my limbs trembled, and before my eyes fiery-red mists were dancing.

"Downstairs I heard doors banging, heard hurried steps lumber up and down the stairs, heard the servants' voices calling my name—I did not stir.

"And when all had become quiet, I stole cautiously down the back staircase, out into the park, in the wildest wilderness of which I crouched down. A peculiar feeling of bitterness and shame agitated me. I felt as if I must take to flight, only never again to have to face that pair of eyes for whose coming I yet had so longingly waited. And then I pictured to myself what, during these moments, was most probably taking place in the house. Papa was sure to have been somewhat helpless at sight of him, for he certainly still felt the effects of that wicked letter ; he was sure also to have resisted a little when he heard him utter his proposal ; but then Martha had appeared—how quickly she has found her strength again, poor ailing creature, who but a few moments ago lay tired to death on the sofa, how quickly she will have forgotten everything that the years have brought of sorrow and sadness—and now they will lie in each other's embrace and *not* remember me.

" And then suddenly a dark feeling of defiance awoke within me. ' Why do you hide away ? ' cried a voice. ' Have you not done your duty ? Is not all this your work ? '

" With a sudden jerk I raised myself up, smoothed back my tumbled hair from my forehead, and with firm tread and set lips I walked towards the house. No sound of rejoicing greeted my ears. All was quiet—quiet as the grave. In

the dining-room I found mama alone. She had folded her hands and was heaving deep sighs, while great tears rolled down as far as her white double chin.

"'That is the result of her emotion,' thought I to myself, and sat down facing her.

"'Wherever have you been hiding, Olga?' she said, this time drying her eyes quite leisurely. 'You must have a few young fowls killed for supper, and set the good Moselle in a cold place. Cousin Robert has come.'

"'Ah, indeed,' said I, very calmly, 'where may he be?'

"'He is speaking to papa in his study.'

"'And where is Martha?' I asked, smiling.

"She gave me a disapproving look for my precociousness, and then said, 'She is in there, too.'

"'Then I suppose I can go at once and offer my congratulations,' I remarked.

"'Saucy girl,' said she.

"But before I could carry out my purpose the door of the adjoining room opened and in walked slowly, as slowly as if he came from a sepulchre, Robert—Cousin Robert, with ashy pale face and great drops of perspiration on his brow.   I felt how, at sight of him, all my blood, too, left my face.   A presentiment of evil awoke within me.

"'Where is Martha?' I cried, hastening towards him.

"'I do not know.'   He spoke as if every word choked him.   He did not even shake hands.

"And then papa came too, after him.

"Mama had got up and all three stood there and silently shook hands like at a funeral.

"'Where is Martha?' I cried once more.

"'Go and look after her,' said papa, 'she will want you.'

"I rushed out, up the stairs to her room.   It was locked.

"'Martha, open the door!   It is I.'

"Nothing stirred.

"I begged, I implored, I promised to make everything right again.   I lavished endearing epithets upon her—that, too, was in vain.   Nothing was audible except from time to time a deep breath which sounded like a gasp from a half-throttled throat.

"Then rage seized me, that I should be every-where repulsed.

"'I suppose I am just good enough to prepare the mourning repast,' I said, laughing out loud, ran to the maids and had six young chickens killed— and even stood by calmly while the poor little creatures' blood squirted out of their necks.

"One of them, a young cockerel, quite desper-ately beat its wings and crowed for very terror of death, while it thrust its spurs at the maid's fingers.

"'Even a poor, weak animal like this resists when one tries to kill it,' I thought to myself, 'but my lady sister humbly kisses the hand that wields the knife against her.'

"The death of these innocent beings might almost be called gay in comparison with the meal for which they served. No condemned criminal's last meal could pass more dismally. Every five minutes some one suddenly began to talk, and then talked as if paid for it. The others nodded knowingly, but I could very well see : whoever heard did not know what he heard, whoever talked id not know what he was talking about.

"Martha had not put in an appearance. When

we were about to separate, each one to go to his room, Robert seized both my hands and drew me into a corner.

"'My thanks to you, Olga,' he said, while his lips twitched, 'for having so faithfully taken my part. Now we will mark a long pause at the end of our letters.'

"'For heaven's sake, Robert,' I stammered, 'however did this come about?'

"He shrugged his shoulders. 'I suppose I kept her waiting too long,' he then said ; 'she has grown tired of me.'

"I was about to cry out : 'That is not true—that is not true!' but behind us stood my father and informed him that, according to his wish, the conveyance would be ready at daybreak.

"'Then I am not to see you any more?' I cried, alarmed.

"He shook his head. 'We had better bid each other good-bye now,' he said, and squeezed my hand.

"Within me a voice cried that he must not depart thus, that I must speak to him at any price. But I bravely suppressed the words that were nearly choking me. And so we once more shook hands and separated.

" I had several things to do yet in the house, and while I put out some coffee and weighed out flour and bacon for next morning's meal, the words were constantly in my ears : ' You must speak to him.'

" Then, as I went, with my candle in my hand, up to my room, I made a detour past his door, for I hoped I might perhaps meet him on the landing ; but that was empty, and his door was closed. Only the sound of his heavy footsteps inside the room was audible throughout the house.

" In Martha's room it was as silent as death. I put my ear to the keyhole ; nothing was audible. She might as well have been dead or flown.

" Terror seized me. I knelt down in front of the keyhole, begged and implored, and finally threatened to fetch our parents if she still persisted in giving no sign of life.

" Then at length she vouchsafed me an answer. I heard a voice : ' Spare me, child, just for to-day spare me !' And this voice sounded so strange that I hardly recognised it.

" I went on my way now, but my fear increased

lest he might set forth with anger and disappointment in his heart, without a word of explanation, without ever having suspected the greatness of Martha's love.

"A very fever burnt within my brain, and every pulsation of my veins cried out to me: 'You must speak to him—you must speak to him!'

"I half undressed and threw myself on the sofa. The clock struck eleven—it struck half-past eleven. Still his footsteps resounded through the house. But the later it was, the more did it grow impossible for me to carry out my resolve.

"What if a servant should spy upon me—should see me stealing into our guest's room! My heart stood still at the thought.

"The clock struck twelve. I opened the window and looked out upon the world. Everything seemed asleep, even from Robert's and Martha's rooms no light shone forth. Both were burying their sorrow and anguish in the lap of darkness.

"With the night wind that beat against the casement, the words droned in my ears: 'You must—you must!' And like a soft sweet melody it coaxed and cajoled at intervals : 'Thus you will see him again—will feel his hand in yours—will hear his voice—perhaps even his laugh ; do you not want to bring him happiness—the happiness of his life?'

" With a sudden impulse I shut the casement, wrapped myself in my dressing-gown, took my slippers in my hand and stole out into the dark corridor.

" Ah, how my heart beat, how my blood coursed through my temples ! I staggered—I was obliged to support myself by the walls.

" Now I stood outside his door. Even yet his footsteps shook the boards. But the noise of his heavy tread had ceased. He had evidently divested himself of his boots.

" ' You must not knock !' it struck me suddenly, ' that would not escape Martha.'

" My hand grasped the door-handle. I shuddered. I do not know how I opened the door. I felt as if some one else had done it for me.

" Before me the outline of his mighty figure——.

" A low cry from his lips—a bound towards me.

Then I felt both my hands clutched—felt a hot wave of breath near my forehead.

"At the first moment the mad idea may have darted through his brain, that Martha had in such impetuous manner bethought herself of her old love—in the next he had already recognised me.

"'For Heaven's sake, child,' he cried, 'whatever has possessed you? What brings you to me? Has no one possibly seen you, say—has no one seen you?'

"I shook my head. He still evidently thinks you very stupid, I thought to myself, and drew a deep breath, for I felt the terrors of my venture were disappearing from my soul.

"He set me free and hastened to make a light. I groped my way to the sofa, and dropped down in a corner.

"The light of the candle flared up—it dazzled me. I turned towards the wall and covered my face. A feeling of weakness, a longing to cling to something, had come over me. I was so glad to be with him, that I forgot all else.

"'Olga, my dear, good child,' he urged, 'speak out, tell me what you want of me?'

"I looked up at him. I saw his swarthy, serious face, in which the day's trouble had graven deep furrows, and became lost in its contemplation.

"'What do you want? Do you bring me news of Martha?'

"Yes, of course, Martha!' I pulled myself together. Away with this sentimental self-abandon! In my limbs I once more felt the firm strength of which I was so proud. 'Listen, Robert,' said I, 'you will not set out at daybreak already.'

"'Why should I not do so?' said he, setting his lips.

"'Because I do not wish it!'

"'All due respect to your wishes, my dear child!' replied he, with a bitter laugh, 'but they alter nothing in my resolve.'

"'So you want to lose Martha for ever?'

"Now I felt myself once more so strong and joyous in my *rôle* of guardian, that I would have taken up fight with the whole world to bring these two together. Foolish, unsuspecting creature that I was!

"'Have I not already lost her?' he replied, and stared into vacancy.

"'What did she say to you to-day?'

"'Why should I repeat it? She spoke very wisely and very staidly, as one can only speak if one has ceased to love a person.'

"'And you really believe that?' I asked.

"'Must I not believe it? And after all, what does it signify? Even if she had retained a remnant of her affection for me, she did well to get rid of it thoroughly on this occasion; it is better thus, for her as well as for me. I have nothing to offer her; no happiness, no joy, not even some little paltry pleasure, nothing but work, and trouble, and anxiety—from year's end to year's end. And added to that, a mother-in-law who is hostile to her, who would make her feel it keenly, that she had come with empty hands.'

"I felt how my blood rushed to my face. I was ashamed, but not for Martha or myself—for I was of course just as poor as she; no, for him, that he should have to speak thus of his own mother.

"'And now say yourself, my girl,' he went on, 'is she not wiser, with such prospects before her, to remain in the shelter of her warm nest, and to send me about my business, as I could never give her anything but unhappiness?'

"He dishevelled his hair and ran about the room the while like a hunted animal.

"'Robert,' said I, 'you are deceiving yourself.'

"He stopped, looked at me and laughed out loud: 'What is it you want of me? Am I perhaps to demand a written confirmation of her refusal, before I betake myself off?'

"'Robert,' I continued, without allowing myself to be put out, 'tell me candidly whether you love her?'

"'Child,' he replied, 'should I be here if I did not love her?'

"With his huge arms outspread he stood before me. I felt as if I must be crushed between them if they closed around me—everything danced before my eyes—I squeezed myself further into my corner. And then there came into my thoughts what I had pictured to myself now and for years before; how I would love him if I were Martha, and how I should want him to love me in return.

"' See, Robert,' I said, 'taking me altogether, I am a foolish creature. But as regards love, I do know about that, not only through the poets; I have felt it in myself for a long time.'

"' Do you love some one then?' he asked.

"I blushed and shook my head.

"' How else can you feel it within you?' he went on.

"' It came as an inspiration from Heaven,' I replied, lowering my gaze to the ground, 'but I know I would not love like you two. I would not be downcast, I would not steal away as you are doing and say: "It is better so!" I would compel her with the ardour of my soul; I would conquer her with the strength of my arms; I would clasp her to my breast and carry her away with me, no matter whither! Out into the night, into the desert, if no sun would shine upon us, no house give us shelter. I would starve with her at the roadside, rather than give fair words to the world—the world that sought to separate me from her. Thus, Robert, I would act if I were you; and if I were she, I would laughingly throw myself upon your breast, and would say to you:

"Come, I will go a-begging for you if you have no bread, my lap shall be your resting-place if you have no bed, your wounds I will heal with my tears—I will suffer a thousand deaths for your sake, and thank God that it is vouchsafed to me to do so." You see, Robert, that is how I imagine love, and not pasted together out of fear of mothers-in-law and unpaid interests.'

"I had talked myself into a passion. I felt how my cheeks were a-glow, and then suddenly shame overwhelmed me at the thought that I had thus laid bare to him my innermost being. I pressed my hands to my face, and struggled with my tears.

"When I dared to look up again, he was standing before me with glistening eyes and staring at me.

"'Child,' he said, 'where in all the world did you get that from? Why it sounded like the Song of Songs.'

"I set my teeth and was silent. I did not know myself how it had come to me.

"He then seated himself at my side and seized both my hands.

"'Olga,' he went on, 'what you just said was not exactly practical, but it was beautiful and true, and has stirred up the very depths of my soul. It seemed to me as if I were listening to a voice from some other world, and I am almost ashamed of having been faint-hearted and cowardly. But even if I braced myself up and thought as you do: what good would it all be, seeing that she no longer cares for me?'

"'She not care for you?' I cried, 'she will die of it, if you leave her, Robert!'

"'Olga!'

"I saw how a joyful doubt illumined his countenance, and I felt as if a strange hand were gripping at my throat; but I would not let myself be deterred from my purpose, and gathering together all my defiance, I continued: 'I know, Robert, that you will despise me when you have heard what I am about to tell you; but I must do it, so that you may understand that you *cannot* depart. I have played a false game towards you, Robert, I have betrayed your confidence.'

"And with bated breath, gasping forth the

words, I told him what I had done with his letters.

" I had not nearly finished when I suddenly felt myself seized in his arms and clasped to his breast.

"' Olga, and this is true ?' he cried, quite beside himself with joy, ' can you swear to me that it is the truth ?'

"I nodded affirmatively, for the tremor that ran deliciously through my veins had robbed me of speech.

"' God bless you for this, you wise, brave girl,' he cried, and pressed me so firmly to his breast that I could hardly draw my breath. I let my head drop upon his shoulder and closed my eyes. And then I started as I felt his lips upon mine. It seemed to me as if a flame had touched me. And again and again he kissed me, quite senseless with gratitude and happiness.

" I kept thinking : ' Oh, that this moment might never end !' And tremor upon tremor shook my frame ; quite limp I hung in his arms. Only once the idea darted through my mind : ' May you return his kisses ?' But I did not dare to do so.

" How long he held me thus I do not know, I

only felt my head suddenly fall heavily against the sofa-ledge. Then the pain awakened me as from a deep, deep dream.

"I lay there motionless and gasped for breath. He noticed it and cried in alarm, 'You are growing quite pale, child; have you hurt yourself?'

"I nodded, and remarked that it was nothing, and would soon pass over. Ah! I knew too well that it would not pass over, that it would be graven in flaming letters upon my heart and upon my senses, that on many a long, cold, winter's night I should find warmth in the glow of this moment, in this glow which was only the reflection of love for another.

"I knew all that, and felt as if I must succumb beneath the weight of this consciousness, but I braced myself up, for I had sufficiently learnt to keep myself under control

"'Robert,' said I, 'I want to give you a piece of advice, and then let me go, for I am tired!'

"'Speak, speak!' he cried, 'I will blindly do whatever you wish.'

"Then, as I looked at him, it made me sigh with mingled pain and bliss, for the thought kept coming to me : 'He has held you in his arms.' I should have liked best of all to sink back once more with closed eyes into the sofa-corner, and simulate fainting a little longer, but I pulled myself together and said : 'I am pretty certain that Martha will not close her eyes to-night, but be on the watch to see you go. She will want to look after you ; and as her room lies towards the garden she will either go into yours or the one adjoining. When you get downstairs wait a little while, and then do as if you had forgotten something, and then — and then——' I could not go on, for all too mighty within me was the sobbing and rejoicing : ' He has held you in his arms.'

"I feared that I should no longer be able to master my excitement—without a word of farewell I turned to take to flight precipitately. When I opened the door—Martha stood before me. She stood there, barefooted, half-dressed, as pale as death, and trembling. She was unable to stir ; her strength probably failed her.

"And at the same moment I heard behind me a glad cry, saw him rush past me and clasp her tottering form in his arms.

14

"'Thank God, now I have you!' That was the last I heard; then I fled to my room as if pursued by furies, locked and bolted everything, and wept, wept bitterly.

*   *   *   *   *

"Over the days that now followed, with their crushing blows of fate, with their lingering sorrow, I will pass with rapid stride. In them I became matured: I became a woman.

"Eight months after that night papa was carried home on a waggon-rack. He had fallen from his horse and sustained grave internal injuries. Three days later he died. In the misery that now beset the household, I was the only one who kept a clear head. Martha broke down feebly, and mama— oh, our poor dear mama! She had been sitting for so many years comfortably and placidly in the chimney-corner, knitting stockings and chewing fruit-jujubes the while, that she would not and could not realise that it must be different now. She spoke not a single word, she hardly shed a tear, but internally the sore spread, and even had the brain fever, which attacked her four weeks later, spared her, her sorrow would still have broken her heart.

" There, now, those two lay in the churchyard, and we two orphans were left helpless in our desolate home, and waited for the time when we should be driven forth. I, for my part, knew which way my path lay, and knew that the future would have nothing to offer me but the hard bread of service ; I did not despair and did not quarrel with my fate. I knew that I possessed sufficient strength and pride to hold my own even among strangers, but it was for Martha—who now less than ever could dispense with love and consolation — that I trembled.

" Her marriage still lay in the far distance ; Robert must not let her wait much longer or she might easily waste away in her misery and one morning silently die out like a little lamp in which the oil is consumed.

" I was not deceived in him. To the funerals he had not been able to come ; but his words of consolation had been there at all times, and had helped Martha over the most trying hours. For me, too, there was sometimes a crumb of comfort, and I eagerly seized upon it like one starving.

"One day he himself arrived. 'Now I have come to fetch you home,' he cried out to Martha. She sank upon his breast and there wept her fill. The happy creature! I meanwhile crept away into the darkest arbour, and wondered whether my heart would ever find a home prepared for it, where it might take refuge in hours of trouble or hours of happiness! I very well felt that these were idle dreams, for the only place in the world—in short, a feeling of defiance awoke within me, of bitterness so great, so galling to my whole nature, that I harshly and gloomily fled my dear ones' embrace, and grew cold and reserved in solitary sadness.

"I was to go with them, was to share the remnant of happiness that still remained for them, and to make a permanent home for myself at my brother-in-law's hearth; but coldly and obstinately I repudiated his offer.

"In vain both of them strove to solve the riddle of my behaviour, and Martha, who fretted because none of her happiness was to fall to my share, often came at nights to my bedside and wept upon my neck. Then I felt ashamed of my hard disposition, spoke to her caressingly as to a child, and did not allow her to leave me till a smile of hope broke through her trouble.

" For a week Robert worked hard in every direction to dispose of our belongings and find purchasers for them. Very little remained over for us ; but then we did not require anything.

" Then, quite quietly, the wedding took place. I and the old head-inspector were the witnesses, and instead of a wedding breakfast we went out to the churchyard and bade farewell to the newly-made graves, whose yellow sand the ivy was beginning to cover scantily with thin trails.

" During the last weeks I had been looking out for a suitable situation. I had received several offers ; I had only to choose. And when Robert, with grave and solemn looks, placed himself in front of me and solicitously asked, ' What is to become of you now, child ? ' with a calm smile I disclosed to him my plans for the future, so that he clapped his hands in admiration and cri ed ' Upon my word I envy you ; you understand how to make your way.'

"And Martha too envied me, that I could see by the sad looks which she fastened on me and

Robert. She herself wished that she might once more have all my unbroken, youthful strength to lay it upon his altar of sacrifice. I kissed her and told her to keep up her spirits, and her eyes with which she looked imploringly up at Robert said : ' I give you all that I am ; forgive me that it is not more.'

" Next morning we set forth ; the young couple to their new home—I to go among strangers.

*　*　*　*　*

" Of the next three years I will say nothing at all. What I suffered during that time in the way of mortification and humiliation is graven with indelible lines upon my soul ; it has finally achieved the hardening of my disposition, and made me cold and suspicious towards every living human being. I have learnt to despise their hatred and still more their love. I have learnt to smile when anguish was tearing with iron grip at my soul. I have learnt to carry my head erect, when I could have hidden it in the dust for very shame.

" The leaden heaviness of dreary, loveless days,

the terrible weight of darkness in sleepless nights, the loathsome dissonance of lascivious flattery, the endless, oppressive silence of strangers' jealousy —with all these I became familiar.

" It was indeed a hard crust of bread that I ate among strangers, and often enough I moistened it with my tears.

" The only comfort, the only pleasure that remained to me, were Martha's letters. She wrote often, at times even daily, and generally there was a postscript in Robert's scrawling, awkward handwriting. Oh, how I pounced upon it! How I devoured the words! Thus I lived through their whole life with them. It was not cheerful— no, indeed not! But still it was life! Often the waves of trouble closed over them ; then both of them, strong Robert and weak Martha, were defenceless and helpless like two children, and I had to intervene and tender advice and encouragement.

" Finally, I had become so well acquainted with their household that I could have recognised the voice and face of each of their servants, of every one of their friends and acquaintances.

"Aunt Hellinger I hated with my most ardent hatred, the old physician I loved with my most ardent love, the insipid set of Philistines who had such a spiteful way of looking at everything, and so exactly reckoned out on their fingers the progress of decay on Robert's estate, I held in iciest contempt. 'Oh that I were in her place!' I often muttered between my set teeth, when Martha plaintively described the little trials of their social intercourse, 'how I would send them about their business, these cold, haughty shop-keepers! how they should crawl in the dust before me, subdued by my scorn and mockery!'

"But her little joys I also shared with her. I saw her ordering and disposing as mistress in and out of the house, saw the little band of willing servants around her, and wished I could have been still gentler and more helpful than she—this angel in human shape. I saw her seated on the sunny balcony, bending over her needlework. I saw her taking her afternoon rest under the great branches of the limes in the garden. I saw her, as she sat waiting for his appearance, dreamily gazing out upon the whirling

snow-flakes, when, outside, his deep voice resounded across the courtyard, and inside, the
coffee-machine was cosily humming.

"Thus I lived their life with them, while for
me one lonely and joyless day joined on to the
next like the iron links of an endless chain.

"It was in the third year that Martha confessed to me that Robert's ardent wish and her
own silent prayer was to be fulfilled—that she
was to become a mother. But at the same time
her terror grew, lest her weak, frail body should
not be equal to the trial which was in store for
her. I hoped and feared with her, and perhaps
more than she, for loneliness and distance distorted the visions of my imagination. Many a
night I woke up bathed in tears; for in my
dreams I had already seen her as a corpse before
me. A memory of my earliest girlhood returned
to me, when I had found her one day, rigid and
pale, like one dead, upon the sofa.

"This vision did not leave me. The nearer the
decisive term approached, the more was I consumed with anxiety. I began to suffer bodily
from the misgivings of my brain, and the strangers

among whom I dwelt—I will not mention them by name, for they are not worth naming in these pages—grew to be mere phantoms for me.

"Martha's last letters sounded proud and full of joyful hope. Her fear seemed to have disappeared; she already revelled in the delights of approaching maternity.

"Then followed three days in which I remained without news, three days of feverish anxiety, and then at length came a telegram from my brother-in-law—'Martha safely delivered of a boy, wants you. Come quickly.'

"With the telegram in my hand, I hastened to my mistress and asked for the necessary leave of absence. It was refused me. I, in wildly aroused fury, flung my notice to quit in her face, and demanded my freedom instantly.

"They tried to find excuses, said I could not be spared just then, that I must at least make up my accounts, and formally hand over my management; the long and the short of it was, that by means of despicable pretexts they delayed me for two days, as if to make the dependant, who had always behaved so proudly, feel once more to the full the degradation of her humble position.

" Then came a night full of dull stupefaction in the midst of the sense-confusing noise of a railway carriage, a morning of shivering expectation spent amidst trunks and hat-boxes in a dreary waiting-room, where the smell of beer turned one faint. Then a further six hours, jammed in between a commercial traveller and a Polish Jew, in the stuffy cushions of a postchaise, and at last—at last in the red glow of the clear autumn evening, the towers of the little town appeared in view, near the walls of which those dearest to me—the only dear ones I possessed in the world—had built their nest.

" The sun was setting when I alighted from the postchaise, between the wheels of which dead leaves were whirling about in little circles.

" With fast beating heart I looked about me. I thought I saw Robert's giant figure coming towards me ; but only a few stray idlers were loafing around, and gaped at my strange apparition. I asked the conductor the way, and, relying for the rest upon Martha's description, I set forth alone on my search.

" In front of the low shop doors, groups were

standing gossiping, and people out for a walk sauntered leisurely towards me. At my approach they stopped short, staring at me like at some wonderful bird ; and when I had passed, low whispers and giggles sounded behind me. A horror seized me at this miserable Philistinism.

"Not until I saw the town gate with its tower-like walls rise up before me, did my mind grow easier. I knew it quite well. Martha in her letters was wont to call it the 'Gate of Hell,' for through it she had to pass when an invitation from her mother-in-law summoned her into the town.

"As I walked through the dark vaulting, I suddenly saw on the other side of the archway, framed as it were in a black frame, the 'Manor' before my eyes.

"It lay hardly a thousand paces away from me. The white walls of the manor house gleamed across waving bushes, flooded by the purple rays of the setting sun. The zinc-covered roof glistened as if a cascade of foaming water were gliding down over it. From the windows flames seemed to be bursting, and a storm-cloud hung like a canopy of black curdling smoke over the coping.

"I pressed my hands to my heart; its beating almost took my breath, so deeply did the sight affect me. For a moment I had a feeling as if I must turn back there and then, and hasten away precipitately from this place, never stopping or staying till the distance gave me shelter. All my anxiety for Martha was swallowed up in this mysterious fear, which almost strangled me. I rebuked myself for being foolish and cowardly, and, gathering together all my strength, I proceeded along the country road in which half-dried-up puddles gleamed like mirrors in the cart-ruts. Through the crests of the poplars above me there passed a hoarse rustling, which accompanied me till I reached the courtyard gate. Just as I entered it, the last sunbeam disappeared behind the walls of the manor and the darkness of the mighty lime trees, which spread from the park across the path, so suddenly enveloped me that I thought night had come on.

"To the right and left tumble-down brickwork, overgrown with half-withered celandine, jutted out above ragged thorn-bushes—the remains of the old castle, upon the ruins of which the manor house had been erected. An atmosphere of death and decay seemed to lie over it all.

"I spied fearfully across the vast courtyard, which the dusk of evening was beginning to cloak in blue mists. At every sound I started; I felt as if Robert's mighty voice must shout a welcome to me. The courtyard was empty, the silence of the vesper hour rested upon it. Only from one of the stable-doors there came the peculiar hissing sound which the sharpening of a scythe produces. A scent of new-mown hay filled the air with its peculiarly sweet, pungent aroma.

"Slowly and timidly, like an intruder, I crept along the garden railings towards the manor house, that seemed to look down upon me grimly and forbiddingly, with its granite pillars and its weather-beaten turrets and gablés. Here and there the stucco had crumbled away, and the blackish bricks of the wall appeared beneath it. It looked as if time, like a long illness, had covered this venerable body with scars. The front door stood ajar. A large dark hall opened before me, from which a peculiar odour of fresh chalk and damp fungi streamed towards me — through small coloured glass windows, placed like glowing nests close under the ceiling and all covered with cobwebs, a dim twilight penetrated this space, hardly sufficient to bring into light the immense cupboards ranged along the walls. A brighter gleam fell upon a broad flight of stairs worn hollow, the steps of which rested upon stone pilasters. High vaulted oaken doors led to the inner apartments, but I did not venture to approach one of them. They seemed to me like prison gates. I was still standing there, timidly trying to find my way, when the front door was torn open and through the wide aperture two great yellow-spotted hounds rushed upon me.

" I uttered a cry. The monsters jumped up at me, snuffed at my clothes, and then raced back to the door, barking and yelling.

" 'Who is there?' cried a voice, whose deep-sounding modulations I had so often fancied I heard in waking and dreaming. The aperture was darkened. There he stood.

" Red mists seemed to roll before my eyes. I felt as if my feet were rooted to the ground. Breathing heavily, I leant against the stair column.

"'Who the deuce is there?' he cried once more, while he vainly tried to pierce the darkness with his eyes.

"I gathered up all my defiance. Calmly and proudly, as I had bid him farewell years before, would I meet him again to-day. What need for him to know how much I had suffered since then!

"'Olga—really—Olga—is it you?' The suppressed delight that penetrated through his words gave me a warm thrill of pleasure. I felt for a moment as if I must throw myself upon his breast and weep out my heart there, but I kept my composure.

"'Were you not expecting me?' I asked, mechanically stretching out my hand to him.

"'Oh, yes—of course—we have been expecting you every hour for the last two days—that is, we began to think——'

"He had clasped my hand in both his, and was trying to look into my face. A peculiar mixture of cordiality and awkwardness lay in his manner. It seemed as if he were vainly trying to discover traces of his former good friend in me.

"'How is Martha?' I asked.

"'You will see for yourself,' he replied. "I do not understand these things. To me she appears so weak and so fragile that I tell myself it will be a miracle if she survives it. But the doctor says she is getting on well, and I suppose he must know best."

"' And the child?' I asked further.

" A low, suppressed laugh sounded down to me through the semi-obscurity.

"' The child—h'm—the child——' and instead of completing his sentence, he gave the dogs a kick, which sent them tearing out of the house forthwith.

"' Come,' he then said, ' I will show you the way.'

" We went upstairs, silently, without looking at each other.

"' You have grown a stranger to him !' I thought to myself, and terror arose within me, as if I had lost some long-cherished happiness.

"' Wait a moment,' he said, pointing to one of the nearest doors. ' I should like to say a word to her to prepare her; the excitement, else, might hurt her.'

15

" Next moment I stood alone in a dark, high-vaulted corridor, at the further end of which the rays of the departing day shone in dark glowing flames, and cast a long streak of light upon the shining flags of the flooring. Undefined sounds, like the singing of a child's voice, floated past my ears, when the draught caught in the arches.

" A low cry of joy, which penetrated to me through the door, made me start up. My blood welled hotly to my heart : I felt as if its rushing must choke me. Then the door opened, Robert's hand groped for me in the darkness. Quite dazed, I allowed myself to be pulled forward, and only recovered myself when I had dropped on my knees at a bedside, burying my face in the pillows, while a moist, hot hand lovingly stroked my head. A feeling of homeliness, soft and soothing, such as I had not known for years, cajoled my senses. I feared to raise my eyes, for I thought it must all be lost to me again if I did.

" Like a blessing from above the hand rested upon my head. Supreme gratitude filled my breast. I seized the hand which trembled in mine and pressed my lips upon it long and passionately.

"'What are you doing there, sister—what are you doing?' I heard her tired, slightly veiled voice.

"I raised myself up. There she lay before me, pale and thin-faced, with dark hollows round her eyes, in which tears were glistening. Like a flake of snow she lay there, so delicate and so white; blue, swollen veins were traceable on her wan neck, and on her forehead, which seemed to shine as with a light from within, there stood beads of perspiration. She was aged and worn since I had last seen her, and it did not seem as if the crisis of the birth alone had acted destructively upon her. But her smile remained the same as of old, that loving, comforting, blessing-dispensing smile, with which she helped every one, even though she herself might be utterly helpless.

"'And now you will not go away again,' she said, looking at me as if she could never gaze her fill; 'you will stay with us—for always. Promise it me—promise it me now at once!'

"I was silent. Happiness had come upon me, burning like a fire from heaven. It tortured me, it hurt me.

"'Do help me to entreat her, Robert,' she began anew.

"I started. I had entirely forgotten him, and now his presence acted upon me like a reproach.

"'Give me time to consider it—till to-morrow,' I said, raising myself up. A dark presentiment awoke within me that here would be no abiding-place for me for long. Such happiness would have been too great for me, unhappy being, whom fate mercilessly drove among strangers.

"I saw that Martha was anxious to spare my feelings.

"'Till to-morrow, then,' she said softly, and squeezed my hand; 'and to-morrow you will have found out how necessary you are to us, and that we should be crazy if we let you go away again; isn't it so, Robert?'

"'Of course—why, of course!' he said, and with that burst into a laugh which sounded to me strangely forced. He evidently did not feel comfortable in the presence of us two. And soon after he took up his cap and showed signs of going off quietly.

"'Won't you show her our child?' whispered

Martha, and a smile of unutterable bliss spread over her wasted features.

" ' Come,' he said, ' it sleeps in the next room.'

" He preceded me. With difficulty he pushed his huge figure through the half-open door.

" There stood the cradle, lit up by the red rays of the setting sun. From among the pillows there peeped a little copper-coloured head, hardly larger than an apple. The wrinkled eyelids were closed, and in the little mouth was stuck one of the tiny fists, its fingers contracted, as if in a cramp.

" My glance travelled stealthily up from the child to its father. He had folded his hands. Devoutly he looked down upon this little human being. An uncertain smile, half-pleased, half-embarrassed, played about his lips.

" Now, for the first time, I was able to contemplate him calmly. The purple evening rays lay bright upon his face, and brought to light, plainly and distinctly, the furrows and wrinkles which the three last years had graven upon it. Shades of gloomy care rested upon his brow, his eyes had lost their lustre, and round about his mouth a twitching seemed to speak to me of dull submission and impotent defiance.

"Unutterable pity welled up within me. I felt as if I must grasp his hands and say to him, 'Confide in me—I am strong; let me share your trouble.' Then, when he raised his eyes, I was terrified lest he should have noticed my glance, and hastily kneeling down in front of the cradle, I pressed my lips upon the little face, which started as if in pain at my touch.

"When I got up I saw that he had left the room.

"Martha's eyes shone in anxious expectation when she saw me. She wanted to hear her child admired.

"'Isn't it pretty?' she whispered, and stretched out her weak arms towards me.

"And when her mother's heart was satiated with pride, she bade me sit down beside her on the pillows and nestled with her head up to my knee, so that it almost came to lie in my lap.

"'Oh, how cool that is!' she murmured, closed her eyes, and breathed deeply and quietly as if asleep. With my handkerchief I wiped the perspiration from her forehead.

"She nodded gratefully, and said: 'I am just

a little exhausted yet, and my limbs feel as if they were broken ; but I hope to be able to get up again to-morrow, and look after the household.'

" ' For heaven's sake, what are you dreaming of ? ' I cried, horrified.

" She sighed. ' I must—I must. It does not let me rest.'

" ' What does not let you rest ? '

" She did not answer, and then suddenly she began to weep bitterly.

" I calmed her, I kissed the tears from her lashes and cheeks, and implored her to pour out her heart to me. ' Are you not happy ? Isn't he good to you ? '

" ' He is as good to me as God's mercy ; but— I am not happy—I am wretched, sister ; so wretched that I cannot describe it to you.'

" ' And why, in all the world ? '

" ' I am afraid ! '

" ' Of what ? '

" ' That I—make him unhappy ; that I am not the right one for him.'

" A sudden icy coldness ran through me. It seemed to emanate from her body upon mine.

" ' You see, you feel it too ! ' she whispered, and looked up at me with great frightened eyes.

" ' You are foolish,' I said, and forced myself to laugh ; but the chillness did not leave my limbs. A dark suspicion told me that perhaps she might be right.   But now it was for me to comfort her !

" ' However could you give way to such silly self-torture ? ' I cried.   ' Does not his behaviour at all times prove to you how wrong you are ? '

" ' I know, what I know,' she answered, softly ; with that obstinacy of endurance which is given as a weapon to the weak. ' And what I am now telling you, does not date from to-day—the fear is years old ; I had it in my heart already before I was engaged to him, and I quite well knew at that time why I refused him—for very love ! '

" ' Martha, Martha ! ' I cried, reproachfully ; ' it seems to me that you concealed a great deal from me.'

" ' At that time I did tell you everything,' she replied.   ' You only would not believe me ; you wanted to make me happy by force, and later— why should I say anything ?   On paper everything sounds so different from what one means ; you might even have thought you discovered a reproach against him or even against yourself, and naturally I could not risk such a misunderstanding growing up. My misery already began on the first day when we arrived here. I saw how he and his mother fell out, and a voice within me cried: "You are the cause of it." I saw how he grew sadder and gloomier from day to day, and again and again I said in my heart: "You are the cause of it." At nights I lay awake at his side, and tortured myself with the thought: why are you so dull and so depressing, and why can you do nothing but cling to him weeping, and suffer doubly when you see him suffering? Why have you not learnt to greet him with a song as soon as he comes in, and with a laugh to kiss away the wrinkles from his brow? And more than this. Why are you not proud, and strong, and wise, and why can you not say to him: Take refuge with me, when you are fainthearted—from me you shall derive new strength, and I will take care that you do not stumble. This is how you would have done, sister—no—do not contradict me; often enough I have imagined how you would have stood there with your tall figure, and would have opened out your arms to him so that he might seek shelter within them, like in a harbour where storms do not dare to enter. . . . But look at *me*,'—and she cast a pitiable glance at her poor, delicate frame, the haggard outlines of which were traceable beneath the coverlet—'would it not sound ridiculous if I were to say anything of the sort? I, who am almost submerged in his arms, so small and weak am I,—I am only here to seek shelter; to give shelter is not in my power. . . . Do you see; all this I have thought out in the long, dark nights, and have grown more and more despondent. And in the mornings I forced myself to laugh, and tried to pass for a sort of cheerful, happy little bird, for this *rôle*, I thought to myself, is the most suitable one for you, and is most likely to please him; but song and laughter stuck in my throat, and I daresay he could see it too, for he smiled pitifully to it all, so that I felt doubly ashamed.'

" She stopped exhausted, and hid her face in my dress, then she continued :

" ' And as that would not do, I tried at least to

compensate him in other ways. You know that all my life I have toiled and moiled, but never have I worked so hard as in these three years. And when I felt myself growing faint and my knees threatened to give way under me, the thought spurred me on again : "Show that at least you are of *some* good to him ; do not ever let him become conscious of how little he possesses in you. . . . But of what avail is it all! My efforts are not the least good. Everything goes topsy-turvy all the same, as soon as ever I turn my back. I am constantly in terror lest one day my management should no longer suffice him."

" Thus the poor creature lamented, and I felt positively frightened at so much misery.

" 'Listen, I have a favour to ask of you,' she begged at last, and clutched my hands ; 'do try and sound him as to whether he is—is satisfied with me, and then come and tell me.'

"I drew her to me ; I lavished loving epithets upon her, and endeavoured to soothe away her fear and trouble. Eagerly she drank in every one of my words ; her feverishly glowing eyes hung spellbound upon my lips, and from time to time a feeble sigh escaped her.

" ' Oh, if I had always had you near me ! ' she cried, stroking my hands. But then a fresh idea seemed to make her despondent again. I urged her, but she would not put it into words, until at length it came out with stuttering and stammering.

" ' You will do everything a thousand times better than I ; you will show him what he *might* have had, and what he *has.* Through you he will finally realise what a miserable creature I am.'

" I was alarmed ; then I felt plainly : my dream of possessing a home was already dreamed out. How could I remain in this place, when my own sister was consuming herself with jealous anxiety on my account ?

" She felt herself that she had pained me ; stretching up her thin arms to my neck, she said : ' You must not misunderstand me, Olga. What I feel is not jealousy; I am so little jealous, that I have no more ardent wish than that you two should become united after my death, and '——

" ' After your death ! ' I cried, in horror. ' Martha, you are sinning against yourself ! '

" She smiled in mournful resignation.

" 'I know that better than you,' she said. 'My vital strength has been broken for a long time. The long waiting in those days already undid me. Now, of course, I thought that with this birth all would be nicely at an end, and that is why I longed so for you, because I wanted first to arrange everything clearly between you two. But, however things may turn out, it won't be long before I have to give in and die, and before then I want to feel sure that I am leaving him and the child in good keeping.'

" I shuddered, and then a sudden lassitude came over me. I felt as if I must throw myself down at the bedside and weep, and weep—weep my very heart out. Then from the next room came the crying of the child, which had woke up and wanted its nurse. I drew a deep breath, and bethought myself of the duty which was imposed upon me.

" 'Do you hear, Martha?' I cried. 'You are ready to despair when Heaven has bestowed on you the greatest blessing that a woman can know? Through your child you will raise yourself up anew; its young life will also bring new strength to yours.'

" Her eyes shone for an instant, then she sank back and smilingly closed her lids. The feeling of motherhood was the only one capable of winging her hope.

" Once more she opened her lips, and murmured something. I bent down to her, and asked: 'What is it, sister?'

" 'I should like to be of some use in the world,' she said with a sigh, and with this thought she fell asleep.

" It had grown pitch dark when Robert entered the room. In sudden fright I started up. A feeling seized me as if I must hide away, and flee from him to the ends of the earth: ' He must not find you; he shall not find you!' a voice within me cried. My cheeks were flaming, and a vague fear arose in me lest their tell-tale glow might gleam through the darkness.

" He approached the bed, listened for a while to Martha's quiet breathing, and then said softly: ' Come, Olga! You are tired; eat something, and go to rest, too.'

" I should have liked to remonstrate, for I was afraid of being alone with him ; but in order not to wake my sleeping sister, I obeyed silently.

" The dining-room was a vast, whitewashed apartment, packed full of old-fashioned furniture, which kept guard along the walls like crouching giants. Under the hanging-lamp stood a table with two covers laid.

" ' I let the household finish their meal first,' said Robert, turning towards me, ' for I did not want to bother you with strange faces.' With that he threw himself heavily into an arm-chair, rested his chin on his hand, and stared into the salt-cellar.

" Why, you are not eating anything ! ' he said, after a while. I shook my head. I could not for the life of me have swallowed a morsel, though hunger was gnawing at my entrails. The sight of him positively paralysed me.

" Renewed silence.

" ' How do you find her ? ' he asked at length.

" ' I do not know,' said I, speaking by main force, ' whether I ought to be pleased or anxious ! '

" ' Why anxious ? ' he asked, quickly, and in his eyes there gleamed an indefinite fear.

" ' She tortures herself——'

" A look of rapid understanding flew across to me, a look which said: 'Do you also know that already? Then he raised his fist, stretched himself and sighed. His bushy hair had fallen over his forehead. The bitter lines about his mouth grew deeper.

" I was alarmed—alarmed at myself. Did not what I had just said sound like an accusation against Martha ; did it not provoke an accusation against her?

" ' She loves you much too much,' I replied, biting my lips. I knew I should pain him, and I meant to do so.

" He started and looked at me for a while in open astonishment ; then he nodded several times to himself and said, 'You are right with your reproach, she does love me much too much.'

" Then I should already have liked to ask his forgiveness again. Surely he did not deserve my malice! His soul was pure and clear as the sunlight, and it was only within me that there was darkness. I felt as if I must choke with suppressed tears. I saw that I could not contain myself any longer, and rose quickly.

" 'Good-night, Robert,' I said, without giving him my hand; 'I am overtired—must go to bed —leave me—one of the servants will show me my way. Leave me—I tell you!'

" I screamed out the last words as if in anger, so that he stopped perturbed. In the cool, semi-obscure corridor I began to feel calmer. For a time I walked up and down breathing heavily, then I fetched one of the maids to show me the way

" 'Mistress arranged everything in the room herself yet, and gave orders that no one was to touch it. There is a letter, too, for you, miss.'

" When I was alone, I held survey. My good, dear sister! She had faithfully remembered my slightest wishes, every one of my little habits of formerly, and had thought out everything that could make my room as cosy and homely as possible. Nothing was wanting of the things which I prized in those days. Over the bed hung a red-flowered curtain exactly like the one beneath the hangings of which I had dreamed

16

my first girlish dreams ; on the window-sill stood geraniums and cyclamen, such as I had always tended, on the walls hung the same pictures upon which my glance had been wont to rest at waking, on the shelves stood the same books from which my soul had derived its first food of love.

"'Iphigenia,' which in those bright calm days had been my favourite poem, lay open on the table. Ah, good heavens! how long it already was since I had read in it, for how long already had I passed it by, because the calm dignity of the holy priestess pained my soul.

"Between the leaves was placed the letter of which the girl had told me. A gentle presentiment, a presentiment of new, undeserved love came over me as I tore open the envelope and read :—

"'MY DARLING SISTER,—When you enter this room I shall not be able to bid you welcome. I shall then be lying ill, and perhaps even my lips will be closed for ever. You will find everything as you used to have it at home. It has

been prepared for you a long time already—
everything was awaiting you. Whether sorrow or
joy may attend you here, lie down to rest in
peace and fall asleep with the consciousness
that you have entered your home. Try and
learn to love Robert as he will learn to love
you. Then all must turn out well yet, whether
God leaves me with you or takes me to Himself.

"'Your sister

"'MARTHA.'

"It was nothing new that she said to me here,
and yet this touchingly simple proof of her love
took such powerful hold of me, that at the first
moment I only had the one feeling, that I must
rush to her bedside and confess to her how unworthy was the being to whom she offered the
shelter of her heart and home.

"For I was no longer in doubt: the ill-fated
passion which I believed I had uprooted from
my soul, had once more profusely sprung into
growth; the wounds, healed up long ago, had
opened anew at the first sight of him; I felt
as if my warm blood were gushing out from them

in streams. Hushing-up and concealment were no longer possible; the vague charm of dawning impressions, the sweet abandon to the intoxication of youth, were things of the past; the bare, glaring light of matured knowledge, the rigid barriers of strict self-restraint had taken their place. Yes, I loved him, loved him with such ardour, such pain, as only a heart can love which has been steeled by the glow of hatred and suffering. And not since to-day, not since yesterday! I had grown up with this love, I had clung to it in secret heart's desire, my whole being had derived its strength from it, with it I stood and fell, in it lay my life and my death.

"What did I care whether he deserved it, whether he understood me! He was not intended to understand it. And not he, it was I who must gain a right to this love. I knew too well at this hour that I should never be able to banish it from my heart. The question was to submit to it, as one submits to eternal fate; but it must not become a sin. It should live on purely, in a pure heart.

"And surely I had not been called in vain to

this house! A mission, a great holy mission awaited me. Martha should perceive forthwith that a beneficent genius was watching over her home. Through me she should learn actively to utilise the love by which she was consumed, for the good of her loved one; through me her courage should be revived and her soul receive new strength. How I would support and comfort her in dark despondent hours! How I would force myself to laugh when a tearful mood troubled the atmosphere! How I would banish the clouds from their gloomy brows with daring jests, and anxiously take care that there should always remain a last little remnant of sunshine within these walls!

"My life should pass away void of desire, happy only in the happiness of my loved ones, discreet, resigned and faithful. I need no longer seek to avoid Iphigenia's image, for the holy and dignified office of priestess was awaiting me also.

"With this pious thought the revolt in my soul disappeared; with it I fell asleep.

"When I awoke on the first morning, I felt contented, almost happy. A holy calm had come over me, such as I had not known since time immemorial. I knew that henceforth I should not have to fear even meeting *him*.

" Martha was still asleep. When I looked through the chink of the door into her room, I saw her lying with her head thrown far back on the pillow, and heard her short heavy breathing.

" I crept away, quite easy in my mind, to take up my office as housekeeper forthwith.

" ' She shall no longer work herself to death,' I said to myself, and rejoiced in my heart. I spent fully an hour going the round of the premises, during which I formally took the management into my hands. The old house-keeper showed herself willing, and the servants treated me with respect. I should anyhow soon have enforced it for myself.

" At the breakfast-table I met Robert. A slight palpitation, which overcame me on entering, ceased forthwith when I bethought myself of my yesterday's vow. Calmly, firmly looking into his eyes, I stepped up to him and gave him my hand.

" ' Is Martha still asleep?' I asked.

"He shook his head. 'I have sent for the doctor,' he said, 'she has passed a bad night— the excitement of seeing you again seems not to have done her good.'

"I felt somewhat alarmed ; but my great resolve had so filled me with peace and happiness, that I would not give way to fear.

"'Will you help yourself?' I asked, 'I should meanwhile like to look after her.'

"When I entered her room, I found her still lying in the same position in which I had left her early in the morning, and as I approached the bed, I saw that she was staring up at the ceiling with wide-opened eyes.

"I called out her name in terror; then a feeble smile came over her face, and feebly she turned towards me and looked into my eyes.

"'Are you not feeling well, Martha?'

"She shook her head wearily, and drew up her fingers slightly. That meant to say: 'Come and sit by me!'

"And when I had taken her head in my arm a shudder suddenly ran through her whole body. Her teeth chattered audibly: 'Give me a warm cover,' she whispered, ' I am shivering so.' I did as she bade me, and once more sat down at her side. She clutched my hands, as if to warm herself by them.

" ' Have you slept well ? ' she asked, in the same hoarse falsetto voice which was quite strange to me in her. I nodded, and felt a hot sense of shame burn within me. What was my grand unselfish resolve, compared with this sort of noble self-forgetfulness, which was evident in every act, however great or small, and was inspired by the same love for everything ? And I even prided myself on my lofty sentiments, conceited egotist that I was.

" ' How did you like the arrangement of your room ? ' she asked once more, while a gleam of slight playfulness broke from her mild, sad eyes.

" In lieu of answer, I imprinted a grateful, humble kiss upon her lips.

" ' Yes, kiss me ! Kiss me once more ! ' she said. ' Your mouth is so nice and hot, it warms one's body and soul through.' And again she shivered with cold.

" A little later Robert came in.

" 'Get yourself ready, my child,' he said, stroking Martha's cheeks, ' our uncle, the doctor, is here.'

" Then he beckoned to me and I followed him out of the room. By the cradle of the new-born babe I found an old man, with a grey stubbly beard, a red snub nose, and a pair of clever, sharp eyes, with which he examined me smilingly through his shining spectacles.

" 'So this is she ? ' he said, and gave me his hand. My blood rushed to my heart ; at the first glance I saw that here was some one who felt as a friend towards me, in whom I might place implicit confidence.

" 'God grant that you have come at a good moment,' he continued, ' and we shall see at once if such is the case. Take me to her, Robert ; I don't suppose it is so bad.'

" I was left alone with the nurse and the child, which restlessly moved its little fists about.

" 'To your happiness also I will earn a claim,' I thought to myself, and stroked the round bare little head, on which a few hardly visible silky hairs trembled. Yesterday I had hardly had a glance for the little being, to-day, as I gazed at it, my heart swelled with unutterable tenderness. 'Thus much purer and better have you grown since yesterday,' I said to myself.

"A long time, an alarmingly long time elapsed before the door of the adjoining room opened again. It was the doctor who came out from it— he alone. He looked stern and forbidding, and his jaws were working as if he had something to grind between them.

"'I have sent him away,' he said, 'must speak to you alone.' Then he took me by the hand and led me to the dining-room, where the coffee-machine was still steaming.

"'I have great respect for you, my young lady,' he began, and wiped the drops of perspiration from his forehead; 'according to everything I have heard about you, you must be a capital fellow, and capable of bearing the pain, if a certain cloven hoof gives you a treacherous kick.'

"'Leave the preface, if you please, doctor,' said I, feeling how I grew pale.

"'Very well! Prefaces are not to my taste either. Your sister'——and now, after all, he hesitated.

"'My sister—is—in—danger—doctor!' I had wished to prove myself strong, but my knees trembled under me. I clutched at the edge of the table to keep myself from falling.

"'That's right—courage—courage!' he muttered, laying his hand on my shoulder. 'It has come—this unwelcome guest—the fever; there is no getting away from it any more.'

"I bit my lips. He should not see me tremble. I had often enough heard of the danger of child-bed fever, even if I could not form for myself any idea of its terrors.

"'Does Robert know?' that was the first thing that entered my mind.

"He shrugged his shoulders and scratched his head. 'I was afraid he would lose his head—I hardly told him half the truth.'

"'And what is the *whole* truth?' Standing up fully erect I looked into his eyes.

"He was silent.

"'Will she die?'

"When he found that from the first I was prepared to face the worst, he gave a sigh of relief. But I did not hear his reply, for after I had, apparently calmly, uttered the gruesome words, I suddenly saw once more before my eyes, with terrible vividness, that vision of my girlish days, when I had found Martha lying like a corpse on the sofa. I felt as if the nails of a dead hand were digging themselves into my breast—before my eyes I saw bloody streaks—I uttered a cry— then I felt as if a voice called out to me :—' Help, save, give your own life to preserve hers !' With a sudden jerk I pulled myself together; I had once more found my strength.

" ' Doctor,' I said, ' if she dies, I lose the only thing I possess in the world, and lose myself with her. But as long as you can make use of me I will never flinch. Therefore conceal nothing from me. I must have certainty.'

" ' Certainty, my dear child,' he replied, grasping my hands, ' certainty there will not be till her convalescence or her last moments. Even at the worst point there may always be a change for the better yet, how much more then now, when the illness is still in its first stage ! Of course she has not much vital strength left to stake— that is the saddest part of it. But perhaps we shall succeed in mastering the evil at its commencement, and then everything would be won.'

" 'What can I do to help?' I cried, and stretched out my clasped hands towards him. 'Ask of me what you will! Even if I could only save her with my own life, I should still have much to make amends for towards her.'

"He looked at me in astonishment. How should he have been able to understand me!

* * * * *

"And now I have come to the hardest part of my task. Since a week I keep sneaking round these pages, without venturing to take up my pen. Horror seizes me, when I consider *what* is awaiting me. And yet it will be salutary for me once more to recall to my memory those fearful three days and nights, especially now, when something of a softer, tenderer feeling seems to be taking root in my heart. Away with it! Away with every cajoling thought which speaks to me of happiness and peace. I am destined for solitude and resignation, and if I should ever forget this, the history of those three days shall once more remind me of it.

* * * * *

"When I pulled my chair up to my sister's bedside to take up my post as nurse, I found she had dropped off to sleep. But this was not the sleep which invigorates and prepares the way for convalescence; like a nightmare it seemed to lie upon her and to press down her eyelids by force. Her bosom rose and fell as if impelled from within and repelled from without. The little waxen-pale, blue-lined face lay half buried in the pillows, across which her scanty fair plaits crept like small snakes. I covered my face with my hands. I could not bear the sight.

"The hours of the day passed by . . . She slept and slept and did not think of waking up.

"From time to time I heard the servants' footsteps as they softly crept past outside—everything else was quiet and lonely. Of Robert no trace.

"At mid-day I felt I must ask after him. They had seen him go out in the morning into the fields, with his dogs following him. So for hours he had been wandering about in the rain.

"As the clock struck three he entered, streaming wet, with lustreless eyes, and his damp unkempt hair matted on his forehead. He must have been suffering horribly. I was about to approach him, to say a word of comfort to him, but I did not dare to do so. The scared, gloomy look which he cast towards me, said distinctly enough: 'What do you want of me? Leave me alone with my sorrow.'

"Clutching at one of the bed-posts he stood there, and stared down upon her while he gnawed his lips. Then he went out—silently, as he had come.

"Again two hours passed in silence and waiting. The carbolic vapours which rose from the bowl before me began to make my head ache. I cooled my brow at the window-panes, and unconsciously watched the play of the dead leaves as they were whirled up in little circles towards the window.

"It already began to grow dark, when suddenly, outside in the corridor, was heard the lamenting and screaming of a female voice—so loud, that even the sleeper started up painfully for a moment. An angry flush flew to my face. I was on the point of hurrying out in order to turn away this disturber of peace, but already at the opened door I came into collision with her.

"At the first glance I recognised this red, bloated face, these little malicious eyes. Who else could it have been but she, the best of all aunts and mothers?

"'At length,' a voice within me cried—'at length I shall stand face to face with you!'

"'So you are Olga,' she cried, always in the same shrill, whining tones, which seemed to yell through the whole house. 'How do you do, my little dear? Ah, what a misfortune! Is it really true? I am quite beside myself!'

"'I beg of you, dear aunt,' said I, folding my arms, 'to be beside yourself somewhere else, but to modify your voice in the sick room.'

"She stopped short. In all my life I shall never forget the venomous look which she gave me.

"But now she knew with whom she had to deal. She took up the gauntlet at once too. 'It is very good of you, my child,' she said, and her voice suddenly sounded as metallic as a war-trumpet, 'that you are so anxious about my poor, ailing daughter; but now you can go—you have become superfluous; I shall stay here myself.'

"'Wait; you shall soon know that you have found your match,' I inwardly cried; and, drawing myself up to my full height, I replied, with my most freezing smile : 'You are mistaken, dear aunt; every *stranger* has been strictly prohibited from visiting my sister. So I must beg of you to withdraw to the next room.'

"Her face grew ashy pale, her fingers twitched convulsively. I think she could have strangled me on the spot; but she went, and good, lacka-daisical uncle, who was always dangling three paces behind her, went with her.

"In sheer triumph I laughed out loud : 'What should you want, you mercenary souls, in this temple of pain? Out with you!'

*   *   *   *   *

"It grew night. Like a streak of fire the last red rays of the setting sun lay over the town, the towers of which stood out black and pointed in the glow. For a long time I watched the fiery

17

clouds, till darkness had buried them also in its lap.

"The clock struck nine. Then the old doctor came. He sat for a long time in silence on my chair, stroked my hand at parting, and said: 'Continue—carbolic—all night!' In answer to my anxiously questioning look, he had nothing but a doubtful shrug of the shoulders.

"From somewhere, two or three rooms away, I heard Robert's voice talking at the old man. This was the first sign that he too was in the proximity of the sick-bed. 'Why ever does he stay outside?' I asked myself; 'it really almost seems as if admission were prohibited.'

"The clock struck ten. Silence all around. The household seemed gone to rest.

"The wind rattled at the garden railings. It sounded as if some late guest wished to enter. Was death already creeping round the house? Was he already counting the grains of sand in his hour-glass?

"Desperate defiance seized me. Without knowing what I did, I rushed towards the door, as if to throw myself in the path of the threatening demon.

"Ill-fated creature, I, that I did not suspect what other demon sat lurking in front of that one, on the threshold!

"A few minutes later Robert entered. Not a word, not a greeting—again only that swift, scared look which once already had cut me to the quick. With his heavy, swaying gait he walked up to the bedside, grasped her hand—that hot, wasted hand, with its bluish nails—and stared down upon it. And then he sat down in the darkest corner, behind the stove, and crouched there for two long, long hours.

"With beating heart I waited for him to address me, but he was as silent as before.

"Soon after midnight he left the room. For a long time yet I heard him walking up and down outside in the corridor, and, at the muffled sound of his tramping footsteps, another night came into my mind, when I had listened, no less trembling in fear and hope, to the same sound. Worlds lay between then and now, and the young, foolish creature who had then hearkened out into the darkness, burning with the desire to help and to sacrifice herself, now appeared to me like a strange, radiant being from some distant, shining planet.

" The footsteps grew less distinct.   He had gone back to his room.

" ' Will he return again ? ' I asked myself, putting my ear to the keyhole.   ' In any case he cannot sleep.'   And I started joyfully when the sound once more increased.

" And then the thought came to me, ' What concern is it of yours whether he returns or not ? Are you here in this place for his sake ?   Is not your happiness, your life, your all, lying here before you ? '

" I fell down by the bedside, and, covering Martha's hands with kisses, I implored her to have mercy—that I wanted to speak to her—that it was bursting my heart-strings—that it was stifling me—that I should suffocate.

" But she did not wake.   Doubled up with pain she lay there, a miserable little heap of bones.   On her cheek-bones were little flaming spots.   Her breath panted.   Once she moved her lips as if to speak, but the words died away in a toneless gurgling.

" What a terrible silence all around !   The clock ticked, along the wall by the casement the wind passed softly moaning, and from the other room sounded the muffled tramp of the wanderer—all else still.

"And suddenly it seemed to me as if in this stillness I heard the blood in my own body seething and boiling.   I listened.   Evidently that was my blood rushing wildly through my veins.

"'Why is its flow not quiet and well-behaved,' I asked myself, 'in accordance with my great resolve ?   Is not this sin torn out with all its roots—burnt out by a thousand purifying fires ?   Do I not stand here as the priestess, void of desire, pure and blessed ? '

"And again I listened !   These are hallucinations, I told myself, and yet I grew afraid at the gushing and rushing, which seemed to increase with every minute.   I saw a stream which carried me away in its torrents—a stream of blood !   A rock with sheer points jutted out from it.   Thereon a word stood written with flaming letters, the word 'Bloodguiltiness.'

"The footsteps grew louder.   I jumped up. . . .

He came, seated himself on the pillow, wiped the perspiration from her forehead with the flat of his hand, and passed his fingers through her hair.

"Stealthily I watched him. I hardly dared to breathe any more. His eyes gleamed bloodshot in their sockets. His lips were pressed together in bitter reproach. He sat there as if petrified with unuttered pain. The desire to approach him shook me like a fit of ague. But when I was on the point of rising, it was as if two iron fists laid themselves upon my shoulders and forced me back on to my chair.

"At length I spoke his name, and was startled, so strange, so weird did the sound of my own voice appear to me. He turned round and stared at me.

"'Robert,' I said, 'why do you not speak to me? You will feel easier if you let some one else share what is oppressing you.'

"Then he jumped up and grasped both my hands. His touch made me feel hot and cold all over. But I forced myself to keep my ground, and firmly looked into his face.

"'That is the first good word that you have vouchsafed me, Olga,' he said.

"'What do you mean by that, Robert?' I stammered. 'Have I been unkind towards you?'

"'Only unkind?' he replied. 'Like a stranger, like an intruder you have treated me, and have driven me from the bedside of my wife.'

"'Heaven forbid!' I cry, and free myself from him, for I feel I am about to sink upon his breast.

"And he continues, 'Olga, if ever I did you any wrong—I know not what, but it must be so, else your look and manner would not be so stern and forbidding towards me—if I did you any wrong, Olga, it was not my fault. I always meant well towards you. I have—you might always have been here like at home; you need never have gone among strangers; and in the presence of that one whom we both love——'

"Why must he mention her name to me? A wild joy had flamed up within me; I felt as if I had wings; then her name struck me like the cut of a whip. I bit my lips till they bled. Indeed I would be calm, would act the guardian angel.

"'Robert,' said I, 'you have been gravely mistaken about me. I never bore you any ill-will. Only I have grown reserved and defiant among strangers. You must have patience with me— must trust me. Will you?'

"Then it broke from his eyes like sunshine. 'I have so much to thank you for already, Olga,' he said; 'how could I do otherwise than continue to trust you? You know, since that day when we rode together into the wood, do you remember?'— ah, did I remember indeed!—'since that day I have loved you like a sister, yes, more than all my sisters. And at the same time I looked up to you and revered you like my guardian spirit. That is indeed what you have been to me. You will be so in future, too, won't you?'

"I nodded silently, and pressed both my hands to my bosom; then, when he noticed it, I let them drop, but I staggered back three paces; it was a miracle that I kept myself upright.

"He stepped up to me in alarm. 'I am tired,' I said, and forced myself to smile. 'Come, we will sit down; the night is long yet.'

"So we both sat opposite each other at the foot of the bed, with the narrow bedstead between us, rested our arms on the ledge, and looked across at Martha's face, which moved with cramp-like twitchings. Her eyelids seemed closed, deep shadows from her lashes fell across her cheeks ; but, on bending down, one could see the whites of the eyes gleaming with a faint sheen, like mother-of-pearl, in their dark sockets. He observed it too.

"'As if she had already died,' he murmured, and buried his head in his hands. 'And if she dies,' he continued, 'she will not die through the child, not through this wretched fever; through my fault alone, Olga, she will perish!'

"'For God's sake, what are you saying?' I cried, stretching out my arms towards him.

" He nodded and smiled bitterly.

"'I have seen it very well, Olga, all through these three years; over and over again it is my fault. First, I left her longing and fearing between hope and despair for seven long years, till the strength was drained in this way from her body and soul—heaven knows she never had much to spare; and then I dragged her with her sickly body and broken spirit here into this misery,

where all were hostile to her, and those most
hostile who should have held her most dear. And
I myself!—yes, if I myself had been brave and of
good cheer, if I could have guarded her that her
foot might not dash against any stone, if I had
spread sunshine across her path, then perhaps she
might have flourished at my side. But I was often
rough and surly, stormed and raged in the house
and the farm, never thinking how every loud word
made her start, so that she already grew pale if I
only frowned. Look at this little handful of life,
how it lies here; and then look at me, the great,
uncouth, coarse-grained giant! Sometimes in the
night when I woke, I was afraid lest I might possibly crush her in my arms. And, after all, I have
crushed her! What I required was a wife, strong
and——'

"He stopped short, terrified, and cast a glance,
which eloquently pleaded for forgiveness, towards
Martha's face, but I completed his sentence for
myself.

"When he had left the room a wild feeling of
joy seized me. It rushed through my head like a
whirlwind; it confused my senses; my pride, my

defiance, my self-respect, everything seemed to be swallowed up in it.

" The atmosphere of the sick room lay heavily upon me, like a suffocating cloth. My brain was burning with the carbolic vapours which rose up from the bowl in front of me. My breath began to fail me.

" I fled to the window, and pressing my forehead against the sash, I drank in the cold night air which found its way into the room through the chinks. Morning dawned through the curtains— cold-grey—enveloped in fog. . . . Faintly gleaming clouds slowly heaved upwards on the horizon and threw a fallow sheen over the dripping trees, which seemed to have grown still more bare overnight.

" What a night !

" And how many, worse than this one, are about to follow? What phantoms, begotten of darkness, born in horror, will rise up before my fevered senses as the nights come on ?

" Shivering, I crept into a corner. I was afraid of myself.

" The hours of the morning passed away, and by degrees I grew calmer. The memory of this night, with its feverish turmoil and pangs of conscience, waxed dim. What I had experienced and felt became a dream. A leaden weariness took possession of me; I closed my eyes and thought about nothing.

"And then came a blissful hour. It was towards ten o'clock when Martha suddenly opened her faithful blue eyes and looked up at me consciously and brightly.

"I felt as if God's eye had turned, full of pity and forgiveness, towards me, the sinner. A pure, holy joy streamed through me. I fell across my sister's body, and hid my face at her neck.

"In the midst of her pain she began to smile, with an effort placed her hand upon my head, and murmured, with hardly audible voice, 'I suppose I have been giving you all a great fright?'

"The breath of her words enveloped me like a peace-bringing chant, and for a moment I felt as if the burden at my heart must give way—but I was unable to weep.

"'How do you feel?' I asked.

"'Well, quite well!' she replied, 'only the sheet weighs so heavily upon me!'

"It was the lightest I had been able to find. I told her so ; then she sighed and said she knew she was a fidget, and I was to have patience with her.

"And then she lay again quite still, and constantly looked at me as if in a dream. At length she nodded several times and remarked : 'It is well thus—quite well!'

"'What is well?" I asked.

"Then she smiled again and was silent. And then the pains returned. She shook all over and clenched her teeth, but she did not utter a complaint.

"'Shall I call for Robert?' I asked, for terror overwhelmed me anew.

"She nodded. 'And bring the child too,' she murmured.

"I did as she had bid. She had the little creature laid on the bed beside her, and looked down at it for a long time. She also made an attempt to kiss it, but she was too weak to do so.

"Even before Robert came she had relapsed into her sleep.

" He gave me a reproachful look, and remarked, ' Why did you not send for me sooner ? '

" ' Believe me, it is better thus,' I answered, ' it would have excited her too much to see you.'

" ' You always seem to know what is best,' said he, and went out, fortunately without noticing the glow which suffused my face at his praise.

" Now she lay there again unconscious—her cheeks red, and her forehead wet with perspiration. And added to that, the gruesome play of her lips ! They kept on twitching and smacking.

" Towards one o'clock the doctor came, took her temperature, and certified a diminution of fever.

" ' That will go up and down many a time yet,' he said ; nor did he enter into our joy over her awakening. ' Do not speak to her when she regains consciousness,' he urged, ' and above all, do not allow her to speak herself. She needs every atom of her strength.'

" Before he left, he fixed his eyes on me for a long time, and shook his head doubtfully. 1

felt how the consciousness of guilt drove the blood to my cheeks. It was as if he could look me through and through.

"... In the afternoon I had fetched myself a book from my room, the first I happened to lay my hands upon and tried to read in it; but the letters danced before my eyes, and my head buzzed as if it were full of bats.

"It was a long time before I could even make out the title. I read 'Iphigenia.' Then, seized by sudden terror, I flung the book far away from me into a corner, as if I had held a burning coal in my hand. Towards evening Martha's pains seemed to grow more intense. Several times she cried out loud and writhed as if in a cramp.

"While I was busying myself about her, during an attack of this sort, the old woman suddenly stood at my side. And as I looked at her with her venomous glance, with her studied wringing of hands, and the hypocritical droop of her mouth, the thought suddenly came to me—

"'Here is one—who is waiting for Martha's death—who is wishing for it.'

" My eyesight seemed dimmed by a red veil, I clenched my fists—I all but flung the accusation in her face. And as I stood in front of her, still quite petrified by the thought, she took hold of my arm, and tried, without much ado, to push me aside, so that she might plant herself at Martha's pillow. Perhaps she hoped to intimidate me by this unceremonious proceeding.

" ' Dear aunt,' said I, removing her hand from my arm, ' I have pointed out to you before already that this is my place, and that no one in the world shall dispute it with me. I urgently beg of you to restrict your visit to the other rooms.'

" ' Indeed ? We will just wait and see, my little one,' she screeched, ' we will just ask the master of the house, who has more to say here, his good old mother, or you, vagabond Polish crew ? '

" And still screeching, she departed.

" In a very fever of rage I paced the room. Even I should not have imagined that this sorrowing mother could so quickly and thoroughly change back again into a fury. It only remained for her to give expression to her inner-most wishes.

"'Oh, if it should be true,' I cried, and horror possessed me. 'To wish for Martha's death! Martha, do you hear, to wish for your death! Whom have you ever hurt? In whose way have you ever stood? Who lives in the world who has ever received aught but love and forgiveness from you? If it were true, if any human being should really be so depraved, and still wander upon earth with impunity—verily, it would make one despair of God and of everything good.'

"Thus I spoke and could not heap enough shame and contumely upon the old woman's head.

"And then it struck me that I had been talking myself into a most unworthy passion.

"But I felt easier through it, I dared to breathe more freely, and when I saw poor, ill-treated 'Iphigenia' lying in the dust, I went and picked it up.

"'What crime have I, after all, committed?' I said to myself, 'that I should need to hide away from my ideal?   Have I done anything but bring comfort to one in despair?   Has a single look, a single word been exchanged, which my sister might not have seen and heard?   If it seethes and burns in my breast, what concern is that of any one, as long as I keep it carefully to myself?'

"Thus I spoke to myself, and considered myself almost justified, even before my own conscience.   Blind creature that I was!

*   *   *   *   *

"And once more the gloaming came, once more the setting sun cast its red light through the windows.

"Martha's face was bathed in a purple glow, in her hair little lights sparkled, and the hand that lay on the coverlet looked as though illumined from within.

"I drew the bed-screen closer around her, so that the flimmering rays should not trouble her.

"Then I saw hanging on the wall a withered ivy wreath, which I had not noticed before, a wreath such as I was wont to send on special occasions for our parents' graves. Perhaps that was where this one, too, came from. At the present moment it appeared as if woven of flames, everything about it lived phantastically. And when I looked more closely, it even seemed to me as if it began to revolve, and to emit a a cascade of sparks, like a real wheel of fire.

"'Dear me, now you are already beginning to see visions,' I said to myself, and tried to gain new strength by pacing up and down. But I felt so dizzy, that I was obliged to hold on to the chairs—I gasped for breath.

"Oh, this smell of carbolic—this sickly-sweet odour! It enveloped my senses, it dimmed my thoughts, it spread a presentiment of death and terror all around.

"Then the old doctor came, looked keenly into my face, and ordered me in his fatherly, gruff manner to go forthwith into the open and get some fresh air. He himself would watch till I returned. And in spite of my remonstrance he pushed me out of the door.

"If I could have guessed what was awaiting

me, no power on earth would have moved me to cross the threshold !

"Now I drew a deep breath as I stepped out into the courtyard. The evening air refreshed me like a cooling bath. The last gleam of daylight was vanishing, and veiled in bluish vapours the autumn night sank down upon the earth.

"The two hunting dogs sprang towards me, and then raced off towards the old castle ruins.

"Unconsciously I followed in their track, walking half in my sleep, for the atmosphere of the sick room was still acting upon my senses.

"A mouldering scent of fading weeds and weather-beaten stones wafted towards me from the brickwork. An old porch spread its arch over me. I stepped into the interior. The walls towered up black all round me, the dark sky looked down upon them with its bluish lights.

"Then not far from me I saw a dark figure, the outlines of which I recognised at once, crouching among the loose stones.

"'Robert!' I call out, astonished.

"He jumped up. 'Olga?' he cried in answer. 'Do you bring bad news?'

"'Not so,' say I, 'your uncle, the doctor, sent me out, and——' then suddenly I feel as if the ground were giving way beneath my feet.

"'Take care!' I hear his warning voice, but already I am sinking, together with the crumbling stones, about a man's length down into the darkness.

"'For Heaven's sake, do not stir!' he shouts after me, 'else you will fall still further down.'

"Half-dazed, I lean against the side of the pit. At my feet gleams a narrow strip of earth, on which I am standing; beyond that it goes down into black, unfathomable depths.

"I see him near me, climbing down after me slowly and carefully on the steps of a flight of stairs as it seems.

"'Where are you?' he shouts, and at the same I feel his hand groping for me.

"Then I throw myself towards him, and cling to his neck. At the same moment I feel myself lifted high up and resting upon his breast. It appeared to me as if my veins had been opened, as if in delightful lassitude I felt my warm life's blood flowing away over me.

"His breath wafted hotly into my face. For a moment it seemed to me as if he had softly kissed my forehead. . . . Then we returned to the manor house without speaking. I moved away from his side as far as I could, but in my heart was the jubilant thought, 'He has held me in his arms.'

"On the threshold of the sick room the old physician came towards us, gave us both his hands and said, 'She is keeping up better, children, than I had expected.'

"Within my heart was rejoicing, 'He has held me in his arms.'

*　　*　　*　　*　　*

"And now that night! Even now every minute stands up like a fury before me, and glares at me with fiery eyes! That night will I conjure up as one calls up spirits from the grave, that their witness may animate anew long forgotten blood-guiltiness! What crime did I commit? *None.* My hands are clean. And on that great morning, when our works shall be tried in the balance, I might fearlessly step up to the Throne of the Most High and say, 'Clothe me in the whitest raiment, fasten upon my shoulders the most delicate pair of swan's wings, and let me sit in the front row, for I have a good voice, which only requires a certain amount of practice to do honour to Paradise!' But there are crimes, unaccomplished, unuttered, which penetrate the soul like the breath of infection, and poison it in its very essence, till the body too perishes under its influence.

"It was a night almost like the present one. The moist autumn wind swept past the house in short gusts, and caught itself in the half leafless crests of the poplars, which bowed towards each other and entwined amid creaking and rustling. Not a star was in the sky; but an undefinable gleaming brought into notice dark masses of torn clouds, which sped along as if in rags. The nightlight would not burn; its flickering flame struggled with the shadows which danced incessantly over the bed and the walls. The ivy wreath hung opposite me, looking black and jagged like a crown of thorns.

"It was about ten o'clock when Martha commenced to be delirious.

"She raised herself up in bed and said in a

clear, audible voice, 'I must really get up now—it is too bad!'

"At first joy suffused my face, for I thought she had regained consciousness. 'Martha!' I jumped up and grasped her hand.

"'I have put everything out in readiness—shirts and stockings and shoes, so that a blind man could find them in his sleep. And you need not take any measurements either—make no compliments—make no compliments.' And all the time she stared at me with glassy eyes, as if she saw a ghost; then suddenly she uttered a piercing shriek and cried, 'Roll the stones away from my body—they are crushing me. Why have you buried me under stones?'

"I took the thinnest sheet I could find and spread it over her in place of the coverlet; but even that brought her no relief. She screamed and talked incessantly, and between whiles she muttered eagerly to herself, like one who is learning something off by heart.

"Like this an hour must have passed. I sat in front of my table and stared at her; for I was in a ferment of terror lest any moment might bring some new, still more horrible development. From time to time, when she calmed down a little, I felt my limbs relax; then I closed my eyes and let myself sink back, and each time I had the sensation as if I were sinking into Robert's arms. But there hardly remained even a dull feeling, as if I were thereby committing any wrong; my weariness was too intense. I also had a sensation as if bubbles were bursting in my head, and roses opening out and always putting forth new wreaths of blossoms ; then again there was a hissing sound from one ear to the other, as if some one had run a fuse right through my head and lighted it.

"In this condition of nervous over-excitement, tossed hither and thither between terrified starting up and relaxation, Robert found me, when, towards midnight, he entered the room. He had intended to lie down on his bed for a short time, and then to watch for the rest of the night together with me ; but Martha's screams had scared him too.

"When I saw him, all my exhaustion was as if wiped away; I felt how a new stream of blood shot through my body, and I jumped up to go towards him.

"'Try to rest a little,' he said, looking down at me with tired, swollen eyes; 'you will require all your strength.'

"I shook my head and pointed to my sister, who was just flinging her hands about, as if in her delirium she were trying to tear me from his side.

"'You are right,' he continued. 'Who could be calm enough to rest with this picture before his eyes.' And then he planted himself with clasped hands in front of the bed, bent down towards her and imprinted a soft kiss upon her wax-like forehead.

"'That is how he kissed me too!' a voice within me cried.

"Thereupon he sat down at the foot of the bed, so close to my chair that the arm which he rested upon the slab of the table almost touched my shoulder.

"With the gloomy brooding of despair he stared across at her.

"'Come to yourself, Robert!' I whispered to him, 'all may be well yet.'

"He laughed grimly. 'What do you mean by

"well"?' he cried; 'that she should remain alive and drag herself about with her sickly frame and crushed spirit, as a burden to herself and to others? Do you not know that these are the alternatives between which we have to choose?'

"A cold shudder ran through my very marrow. But at the same time I felt as if the walls were giving way and an unbounded, shining vista opening out before me.

"'Were you not going to be a priestess in this house?' a warning voice within me remonstrated, but its sounds were deadened by the surging of my blood.

"'What is the use of struggling against fate?' he continued; 'I have long since learnt to submit quietly when blow after blow falls down upon me from above. I have become a miserable, weak-minded fellow. I have allowed fate to bind me hand and foot, and now, even if I struggle till the blood spurts from my joints, it is no good! I am powerless and shall remain so, and there's an end of it! But I do not care to talk myself into a passion. Such helpless rage is more contemptible than hypocritical submission.'

"A desire darted through me to throw myself down in front of him, and to cry out to him, 'Do with me what you will: sacrifice me, tread me under-foot, let me die for you; but be brave and have new faith in your happiness——' then suddenly a moan from Martha's lips struck upon my ears, so plaintive, so pitiable that I started as if struck by the lash of a whip.

"I felt ready to scream, but fear of him choked my utterance—only a groan escaped my breast, which I forcibly suppressed, when I noticed how anxiously he was looking into my eyes.

"'Take no heed of me!' I said, forcing myself to smile; 'the chief thing is for her to get better.'

"He crossed his arms over his knee and nodded a few times bitterly to himself. And then again the moaning ceased.

"She had bowed her head upon her breast, and half closed her eyes. One might almost have thought her asleep; but the muttering and chattering continued. There was utter silence in the half-darkened room. Only the wind sped past the window with low soughing, and between the planks of the ceiling the mice scampered about.

"Robert had buried his head in his hands, and was listening to Martha's weird talking. Gradually he seemed to grow quieter, his breath came more regularly and slowly, now and again his head dropped to one side, and next moment jerked up again.

"His sleepiness had overpowered him. I wanted to urge him to go to rest; but I was afraid of the sound of my own voice, and therefore was silent.

"More and more often did the upper part of his body sway to one side, now and again his hair touched my cheek—and he groped about seeking to find some support.

"And then, suddenly, his head fell upon my shoulder, where it remained lying. My whole body trembled as if I had experienced some great happiness.

"An invincible desire possessed me to stroke the bushy hair that fell across my face. Close to my eyes I saw a few silver threads gleaming.

"'It is already beginning to get grey,' I thought

to myself, 'it is high time that he should taste what happiness is like.'　And then I really stroked him.

"He sighed in his sleep and sought to nestle closer with his head.

"'He is lying uncomfortably,' I said to myself; 'you must move up nearer to him.'

"I did so.　His shoulder leant against mine, and his head fell upon my breast.

"'You must put your arm round him,' a voice within me cried, 'otherwise he will still not find rest.'

"Twice or three times I attempted, and as often I drew back.

"What if Martha should suddenly wake!　But even then her eyes saw nothing—her ears heard nothing.

"And I did it.

"Then a wild joy seized me : secretly I pressed him to me—and within me there arose the jubilant thought : 'Ah, how I would care for you and watch over you ; how I would kiss those wicked furrows away from your brow, and the troubles from your soul!　How I would fight for you with my virgin

strength and never rest till your eyes were once
more glad, and your heart once more full of sunshine ! But for that——I looked across at Martha.
Yes, she lived, she still lived. Her bosom rose
and fell in short, rapid gasps. She seemed more
alive than ever.

" And suddenly it flamed up before me, and the
words seemed as if I saw them distinctly written
over there on the wall—

"' *Oh, that she might die !* '

" Yes, that was it, that was it.

" Oh, that she might die ! Oh, that she might
die ! "

VII.

DRAWING a deep breath, the physician stopped short, and wiped the perspiration from his forehead.

Robert had jumped up, stared for a moment at the flaming orb of the lamp, as if dazzled by the light, and then rushed towards the old man as if to tear the paper out of his hands.

"That does indeed stand there?" he stammered.

"Read for yourself!" said the other.

A long silence ensued.

The lamp burnt with its quiet, cheery light as if it were illumining a deed of brightest gladsomeness, and softly, as if with velvety paws, the wind touched the windows. Downstairs everything seemed to be growing quieter. The intervals between the bursts of laughter grew longer and longer—the babel of voices changed to a steady, dull buzz. The people were getting tired—they were digesting.

The physician looked round for Robert. He had dropped down once more upon the ledge of the empty bedstead, had buried his face in his hands, and was absolutely motionless.

Only his heaving breath, which escaped his breast in short, irregular gasps, testified to the turmoil that was raging within him.

" Come to yourself, my boy," said the physician, laying his hand on Robert's shoulder.

" Uncle, of course it goes without saying—she was not in her right mind when she wrote this ? "

" She was never more in her right mind than at that moment "

" How dare you affirm such a thing ? Do not insult the dead ! "

" Nothing is further from my thoughts, dear boy. Who shall presume to cast the first stone at her ? But if you have been listening attentively, you will certainly understand that her whole life was nothing more than the maturing of this moment. Already in her girlish dreams the seeds

19

of this criminal wish lay buried; they put forth sudden shoots on yonder stone in the wood, and came into blossom at the very hour when she crept into your room to unite you with Martha."

"Why did she do that, if she herself wished to step into Martha's place?"

"She was not conscious of what she wished. All her efforts to make you and Martha happy were nothing further than the secret struggle which her pure honest nature was waging with the wish growing up within her, since that day of her girlhood when she had seen you again. But she did not know it. Even her love for you did not become clear to her till she entered your house. How much less then could she suspect what was slumbering, as the fruit of this love, within her soul."

"And yet you say she fought against it and tried to exterminate it?"

"Not spiritually, not consciously. Her thought remained pure till that terrible midnight hour. It was only her instinct which struggled against the poison. That drew new resources daily from the healthy depths of her strong nature, by which to secrete the putrid matter or at least to enclose it so that it became innocuous. For this reason she condemned herself to exile, for this reason even in face of your house she contemplated a hasty retreat. How little she was, even later, conscious of the processes which for years had been developing within her, you may see by the whole tone of her reminiscences. She absolutely unconsciously dwells upon many unimportant incidents, which have nothing to do with the progress of the story and yet are valuable as showing the gradual development of her wish. She knows not why she does so: her feeling alone tells her: this has some connection with my guilt."

"I believe in no guilt!" exclaimed Robert, in greatest excitement. "If that wish was not a mere hallucination, not the result of a momentarily morbid, over-strung frame of mind, but had lain for a long while dormant in her nature, how came it that, only six hours before uttering it, she expressed herself with such indignation about my mother because she suspected her of harbouring it?"

"For my part," replied the old man, "nothing is

more convincing for my view of the matter, than this very indignation. To free her own conscience from the burden which she felt resting upon it, she cast every stone which she could take hold of, at your mother. It was terror at her own sin which drove her to it."

"And the noble, self-sacrificing resolve which she formed only a few days before?"

Over the old man's weather-beaten features there flitted a smile full of understanding and forgiveness.

Then he said, "The old proverb about the good intentions with which the path to Hell is paved, may hold good here too ; but it only touches the surface of the matter. This resolve was a last abortive attempt to unite sisterly love with her longing for you, to make a pact between her powerful, burning desire for happiness and the impulse to keep faith towards her sister. It was the most unnatural thing she could hit upon, for silent resignation was not in her line. It was a particularly cruel fate which doomed her, with her noble disposition and powerful will, to be forced into a sin which is the most common and most cowardly on earth, a sin which I have found lurking on countless faces, when I stood at the bedside of people seriously ill. This, my boy, is one of the darkest spots in human nature, a remnant of bestiality which has managed to find its way into our tamed world; even such sensitive natures as Olga may fall a prey to it, though of course they perish through it, while coarser souls simply conceal and suppress what is struggling to appear from the darkest depths of their beings. Wait, I will speak more plainly. I once came to the bedside of a rich old man, a landowner, whose last breath was not far off. At the head of his bed stood his eldest son, a man of about forty, who for long years had held the post of inspector on strange estates, and whose intended bride was beginning to grow old and faded with waiting. The son was a good, honest fellow who would not have hurt a fly, who loved his father with all his heart, and would certainly have been ashamed to wish his deadliest enemy any ill; but in the stealthy, terrified glance with which he watched me, while I bent down my ear towards the old man's breast, I distinctly read the wish! 'Oh, that he might die!' Another time I was called in to a woman who was very happy in second marriage. Only one cloud troubled her new happiness. Her husband could not befriend himself with the child of her first marriage. He knitted his brows at the mere mention of the little creature, and as she loved him passionately, she feared he might come to hate her on the child's account, and hid it away from him as much as ever she could. The child got scarlet fever. I found the mother kneeling at its bedside and weeping bitterly. She trembled in fear for the feeble little life. Had she not herself brought it forth! Then her husband entered the room—she started—and in the restless, wavering glance which she cast towards the cradle, there stood clearly and legibly written: 'It would be for my happiness, if you died.' I could give you innumerable examples where jealousy, covetousness, desire for independence, restlessness, impulse for liberty, amorous longing, have matured this terrible, criminal wish, which suddenly rises up dark and gigantic within the human breast, in which hitherto only love and light have found a place. Happily nowadays it does not do much harm. In olden, more barbarous times, when the passions were permitted to rage unfettered, the deed aided the thought. And if perchance in the family circle any one happened to be in the other's way, poison and the dagger simply claimed their victims. History and literature abound with murders of this kind, and that great student of mankind, Shakspeare, for example, knows hardly any other tragic motive besides murder of kin. To-day people have grown calmer, and if a struggle for existence happens nowadays to creep into the hòly family circle, one is content to wish the obnoxious one, in a dark hour, six feet under the earth. This wish is the ancient murder restrained by modern civilisation. There, my boy, now I have given you a long discourse, and if, meanwhile, your blood has cooled down, my object is fulfilled."

"So you absolutely condemn her?" Robert anxiously stammered forth.

"My dear boy, I condemn no one," replied the old man, with a serious smile, "least of all such an honest nature as Olga was. The fact alone that she had the courage to confess to herself and to

him whom she loved most, what she was guilty of,
raises her above the others. For this wish, of
which we are speaking, as it is the most hideous
spiritual sin of which the human soul can become
guilty, so it is also the most secret. No friend con-
fides it to a friend, no husband whispers it in the
darkness of the nocturnal couch to his wife, no
penitent dares to confess it to his spiritual adviser,
even the prayer that struggles upwards to heaven
out of the depths of contrition, passes it over in
hypocritical silence. God may have knowledge of
everything, only not of this baseness. Let this
perish in shame and silence, as it was brought
forth in night and horror. And more than this !
This wish is the only crime for which there is com-
monly no expiation, no punishment either before
the tribunal of the outer world, or one's own conscience. This is a case in which even that merci-
less judge which a man carries about within him
proves amenable to bribery. Thousands of people
who have once been guilty of this baseness go on
living happily, put on flesh in perfect peace of soul,
and rejoice in the fulfilment of their wish, which
they themselves forget as speedily as possible, as

soon as ever it is fulfilled. It becomes absorbed into the soul, just as a germ of disease becomes absorbed as soon as the stimulant of disease has disappeared. It is lost without any trace, it is absolutely blotted out by an abundance of social and personal virtues. I on no account say that I condemn these people. What would become of the world if every one who on looking into the glass discovered a wart on his face, were to cut his throat in despair at the fact? The people I have described to you are the healthy every-day people, whose so-called good constitution can stand a blow, and who care not a rap if now and again something objectionable sticks to them. Olga was moulded of finer clay, her nervous system was sensible to lesser shocks, and what only caused others a slight irritation, was to her already a lash of the whip. Such natures are often somewhat morbid, they incline towards melancholy and hysteria, and their soul-life is governed by imaginations, which, in the eyes of others, are apt to assume the character of fixed ideas. And yet everything about them is strictly normal, indeed their organism works even more accurately than that of the ordinary, average human being, and if one were to place them, like delicate chemical scales under a glass case, one might see them work wonders. As a rule a certain weakness of purpose cleaves to this class of sensitive people, which makes them shyly retreat into themselves at the slightest extraneous touch—and this is lucky for them ; for thus they are saved all violent collision with the outer world, to which they would not, after all, prove equal. But woe to those among them who are driven by some impetuous desire, some mighty passion, straight among rocks and thorns! Then it is very possible that an adhering thorn, which others would hardly have noticed, may become to them a poisoned arrow, and corrode their body and soul till they perish in consequence. There, now, I have talked enough. Here lie two or three more sheets. Listen! Here we shall learn how one may be ruined by a wish."

VIII.

"OF that which now followed, I have only retained a vague recollection. I remember that I suddenly uttered a shriek, which made even Martha start up, that I flung myself down at her bedside, clutched her burning hands, and continued to cry out, 'Save me! save me! wake up!'

"And then again I find myself in a different room, into which Robert has taken me. I remember how, there, in the looking-glass, I recognised my distorted face, bathed in the perspiration of terror, how I burst into a laugh, and, shuddering at my own laughter, sank all in a heap, and how all the while, chuckling and hissing with a thousand covetous voices, there came sounding in my ears the wish: 'Oh, that she might die!' How shall I describe it all, without being hunted to death by the spectres of that night?

"The only clear remembrance that I still retain

is that suddenly the doctor's dear old face was bending over me, that I had to drink something that tasted bitter, and—then I know nothing more.

    *   *   *   *   *

" When I awoke the pale light of dawn gleamed through the windows. My head ached, I looked around dazed, and then it seemed as if I saw written on the whitewashed wall opposite, the words: 'Oh, that she might die!'

" I shuddered, and then the thought rose within me: ' Now, if she dies, it will be your wish which has murdered her.'

" I pulled myself together, and walked up to the looking-glass.

" ' So this is what a woman looks like who wishes her sister might die!' said I, while my ashen-pale face stared back at me ; and, seized with a sudden loathing, I hit at the glass with my fist. My knuckles bled, but it did not break. Fool that I was, not to know that henceforth all the world would only be there to hold up a mirror to my crime!

" ' But perhaps she may not die!' it suddenly darted through my brain. Such radiance seemed to burst forth from this thought, that I closed my eyes as if dazzled.

" And then again it cried aloud within me : ' She will die ; your wish has murdered her ! ' I ground my teeth, and groping along by the walls, I crept into the sick room.

" When I stood at the door, and no longer heard any sound from within, the idea took possession of me :

" ' You will find her as a corpse.'

" No, she still lived, but death had already set his mark upon her face.

" The bridge of the nose had become more prominent, her lips no longer closed over her irregular teeth, her eyes seemed to have sunk right down into their dark sockets.

" At her feet stood Robert and the old doctor. Robert had pressed his hands to his face. Sobs shook his frame. The old man scrutinised me with a penetrating glance. Again, for a moment, I felt as if he were looking me through and through, as if my guilt were openly exposed before him. But then, as he hastened towards me, who was tottering, and held me upright in his arms, I recognised that it was only the physician's glance with which he had examined me.

"'How long will she live yet?' I asked, closing my eyes.

"'She is dying!'

"At that moment something within me grew rigid, turned to stone. At that moment hope died within me, and with it my faith in myself, in happiness, in goodness. A great calm came over me. Death, which hovered over this bed, had spread its dark pinions around my body too. With the clear vision of a prophetess, I saw what yet remained to me of life, spread out unveiled before my eyes. Like one dead I should henceforth have to wander upon earth, like one dead I should have to cling to life, like one dead see that happiness approach me, which was for ever lost to me. Robert stepped up to me and embraced me. I calmly suffered it, I felt nothing more.

"Then I sat down close to my sister's bedside, and looked at her, waiting for her death.

"Attentively I followed every symptom of her slow expiring. I felt as if my consciousness had separated itself from me, as if I could see myself sitting there like a stone figure, staring into the dying woman's face.

"No feverish illusion, no morbid self-incrimination any longer disturbed the course of my ideas. It was by this time clear to me that my wish could not in reality bring death upon her, and yet—for me and my conscience it remained the wish alone which had killed her.

"Thus I sat, as her murderess, at her bedside, and waited for her death which was also mine.

"It was a long time coming. The hours of the day passed and she still lived. Her pulse had long ceased to beat, her heart seemed to stand still, and yet her breath continued to come and go in short feeble gasps. While I was lying in a morphia sleep, they had given her as a last resource an injection of musk to revive her strength once more. This was what she was existing on now. But the odour of musk, mingling with the carbolic vapours, filled the room like some heavy, tangible body, weighed on my brow and seemed to crush my temples. I felt as if with every breath I were drinking in increasing burdens.

"In the afternoon Robert's parents came. I,

who had yesterday shown my aunt only pride and contempt, to-day kissed her hand in humiliation. This was the beginning of the penance which I had inflicted upon myself at Martha's death-bed, and which shall endure as long as I live.

"Evening came on. Martha still continued to breathe. With wide-open mouth, her dead eyes covered with a film, she stared at me. Her body seemed to get smaller and smaller, quite shrunk together she lay there. It almost looked as if in death she did not venture to take up even the small space which she had occupied during her lifetime.

"Aunt filled the house with her loathsome sobbing, and the others, too, were weeping ; I alone remained without tears.

"When towards eleven o'clock she had drawn her last breath, I fell into a delirium.

*   *   *   *   *

"Just now I have returned from the manor.

"He was good and kind towards me, and in his eyes there gleamed a half-hidden, bashful tenderness, which my soul drank in eagerly. I feel as if a new spring-time must be coming, my heart is full

of smiles and laughter, and when I close my eyes
golden sunlight rays seem to be dancing round
about me. But now away with this enervating
dream of happiness!

" If he should learn to love me, all the worse for
him! I gave him no occasion—no, indeed not!
I should feel I must despise myself like a very
prostitute if I had done so. Since my convalescence I have managed his household for him
truly and faithfully, for more than a year, without
claiming his approval, without wishing to grow
indispensable to him. Even my dear aunt has
had to recognise that, who almost forces her hospi-
tality upon me, in spite of my being personally so
hateful to her. She is much too good a housekeeper herself not to know that, but for me, the
household would have gone to rack and ruin in
those days, when Robert forgot everything in
gloomy mourning for his dead—not even taking
any interest in the child, which she had left him
as a pledge. But for me, the poor little thing
would be lying under the ground long ago. I will
not enumerate all I did and worked during this time.
It is surely not meet for me to play the Pharisee.

20

" Nor will I speak of expiation. How pompous the word sounds, and what miserable self-deception generally hides behind it ! How shall I wash away what defiles me ? One may expiate some tragic guilt, one can even expiate some great crime, but a piece of baseness such as I committed, cleaves to the soul for ever ! Ah, if I did not know what secret desire lurks in the depths of my heart !

" Why else should I require to stand there absolved before my own conscience, if not in order that I might one day become his ? As if everlasting fate itself had not reared up a wall between us, reaching up from the depths of *her* grave as high as the stars.

" And if some demon should ever whisper into his ear, advising him to stretch out his hand for me, what else could I do but repulse him, as if for his audacity ? But he will never do such a thing. I have succeeded in keeping him at a distance. Let him believe that I have a poor opinion of him, let him believe that I am haughty and unfeeling through self-love. I shall know how to guard my heart's secret.

" If only one thing were not so !

"Sometimes, especially at night, when I am staring into the darkness, a wild, mad longing comes over me with such power, that I feel as if I must succumb to it. It seizes me like a feverish delirium; it dims my senses, and makes my blood boil in my veins; it is the longing to lie just for once upon his breast, and there to weep my heart out. For in those nights my tears were dried up. I have never been able to weep since the day when I found Martha lying on her sick-bed.

*   *   *   *   *

"A fortnight later.

"It has come to pass. He loves me. He came to woo me. Now I know that there is an expiation! These tortures must indeed purify! Jesus, I have lost my childish faith in Thee, but Thou wast a man, Thou hast suffered like me. Thee I implore — no, this is madness! Come to your senses, woman; pull yourself together. Is there not an everlasting resting-place, whither you may flee by your own free will, if your strength is no longer equal to the misery of this life? Who is to prevent you?

"He loves me. I have attained it. But in order

that he might love me, Martha had first to perish, I myself had to sink down into an abyss of guilt and shame from which no power in heaven or on earth can save me.

" I am dead. Dead shall be my desires and my hopes, and my rebellious blood, which wells up seething at thought of him. I will soon compel it to be calm ; and if not——.

"Oh, how he stood before me, timidly stammering forth word by word. How shyly and imploringly his eye sought mine, and yet how he hardly dared to raise his glance from the ground. How, in his awkwardness, he twisted the ends of his beard round his fingers, and stamped his foot when he could not find the right word ! Oh, my poor dear, big child, did you not see how my every limb was trembling with the desire to rush towards you and hold you tight for all eternity, did you not see how my lips were twitching with the temptation to press themselves upon yours, and to hang there till their last breath ?

" Did you not see all this ?

" Did you really believe the words, which half unconsciously I spoke to you ? My heart knows nothing of them, that I swear to you. I have loved you ever since I can remember. I know that my last breath will utter your name.

" And shame on you, if you really had faith in my pretexts ! I leave you for a rich girl ! You, for whom I would gladly beg in the streets, for whom I would work till my eyes grew dim and my fingers sore, if you needed it !

"Do you remember that night in our parents' house, when you were wooing Martha ? Do you remember it and dare to insult me by putting faith in my miserable excuses ?

" And when at parting I gave you my hand, why did you look into my eyes so sadly and humbly ? Did you not know that now that look will haunt me day and night like the reproach of some heavy crime I have committed towards you ?

"No, my friend, you are the only one on earth who have nothing to reproach me with. Towards you I have acted honestly—and most honestly to-day, even though you were never so unutterably deceived as to-day ! If only I might tell you how much I love you ! How gladly would I die in that self-same hour. Only once to lie upon your breast

—only once to hide my head upon your shoulder and weep, weep—weep blood and tears !

" You must never again look at me like that, my giant, as if I had had a right to despise you, as if you were too simple and not good enough for me. I do not know what I might not do in that case! Heaven protect you from me and my love !

*　　　*　　　*　　　*　　　*

" A week later.

" And now I have done it *after all !* I have thrown myself upon his neck ; I have satiated myself with his kisses; I have wept my fill in his arms!

"I am calm—quite calm. I have tasted whatever of happiness life had left to offer me, the sinner.

" But what now ?

" Since hours I have been face to face with the last great question : ' Shall I flee or die ? '

" One or the other I must do this very night ; for to-morrow he will come to lead me to Martha's grave.

" Rather than follow him thither, I will die !

" But I will even assume that I could be enough of a hypocrite not to drop down beside the grave and confess all to him, I will assume that I should not be choked with loathing of myself, that I should really have enough wretched courage to become his wife ; what sort of a life should I lead at his side ?

"What is the good of clinging to happiness when one has long since forfeited it ? Should I not slink about like some poor criminal in her last hours, everlastingly tortured by the fear of betraying myself to him, and yet filled with the desire to proclaim my guilt to the whole world ? How could I sleep in the bed out of which I wished her into her grave ! How could I wake between the walls on which there still stands written in flaming letters : 'Oh, that she might die ! '

" I will converse quite calmly and sensibly with myself, as is meet for one who is making up the account of her life. That I cannot become his wife I know very well.

" Shall I flee ?—What should I do among strangers ? I know them. I know these people and despise them. They have wrought evil towards me ; they would torment me again in the future.

" All the faith, all the love, all the hope still

remaining to me, have their foundation in him alone.

"So I must die! The bottles of morphia stand, well preserved, in the corner of my cupboard. I had some suspicion that I might want them, when, in defiance of the old doctor, I secretly saved up their contents. The few hours of sleep which I thereby lost, will now be amply compensated for.

"Only a letter yet to my uncle the doctor; he shall be my heir and my confidant. Perhaps he can help me to wipe away all traces of my deed, so that Robert may suspect nothing. Not a greeting to him. That is the hardest of all, but it must be so.

*   *   *   *   *

"I have run out secretly and posted the letter. The watchman was signalling midnight. How empty, how dark is the whole world! In the lime-trees the wind is soughing. Here and there a light is sadly gleaming as if to illumine hidden sorrows. A drunken fellow came shouting along the road and made as if to attack me. Darkness, poverty, and brutality out there—in here guilt and unappeasable longing—that would be my future. Verily this life has nothing more to offer me.

"People talk and write so much about the terror of death. I feel nothing of it. I am content, for I have wept my fill. Those suppressed tears weighed heavily upon me; and weeping makes one weary, they say. Good-night!"

THE END.

www.ingramcontent.com/pod-product-compliance
Lightning Source LLC
Chambersburg PA
CBHW031038120726

47905CB00007B/2228